BOOK NEWS

Sign up for exclusive updates and offers at
news.jljarvis.com

GET THE AUDIOBOOK

jljarvis.com/moonlight

MOONLIGHT ON MARINER'S BLUFF

MOONLIGHT ON MARINER'S BLUFF

WATERFRONT SUMMERS
BOOK 3

J.L. JARVIS

Moonlight on Mariner's Bluff

ISBN (ebook) 978-1-942767-87-9
ISBN (paperback) 978-1-942767-88-6

Published by Bookbinder Press
bookbinderpress.com

CHAPTER ONE

SHE BOUGHT a house she'd never seen, in a place she'd never been, based on a real estate photo that made her heart soar. Eight hours north of Manhattan, Nora Delaney stood before the Captain's Watch and wondered if she'd driven straight into the best decision she'd ever made or the biggest mistake of her life.

Sitting atop Mariner's Bluff, the Victorian mansion rose before her, clad in weathered cedar shingles silvered by decades of salt air and storms. Porches wrapped around the structure on two levels with ornate gingerbread trim catching the August light that found its way through the oak leaves. A widow's walk crowned the house like a tiara, its white railings stark against the brilliant blue sky.

Nora pulled the keys from the pocket of her jacket with trembling fingers, which she wanted to blame on the crisp Maine air, but she knew it was nerves. Her red Mini Cooper looked absurdly small parked in the circular drive, dwarfed by the towering house and the ancient oak trees that stood sentinel around it. The moving company was due to arrive the next day. Until then, for the first time in her new home, she would be alone.

She approached the front door, with carved oak panels that seemed to glow in the afternoon light. Each detail drew her artist's eye—the brass hardware green with age, the stained-glass panels casting jeweled reflections across the porch boards, and the shadows. The real estate photos hadn't shown the way shadows seemed to gather in the corners of the wraparound porch or how the widow's walk appeared to shift slightly in her peripheral vision—as if someone had just stepped back from the railing.

The brass key turned easily in the ornate lock, but the heavy door protested with a long, mournful creak as it swung open, as if it were guarding secrets within its weathered walls. Nora stepped inside.

And froze.

The scent hit her immediately—warm and comforting vanilla, cinnamon, and yeast—as if someone had just pulled a fresh batch of pastries from the oven. But the house had been empty for months. She distinctly remembered Milt mentioning that.

Milt, her contractor, had been sending her photos and updates for weeks as he'd worked on the renovations, but they hadn't even discussed scent diffusers. She loved it, but he should have mentioned it first. They would need to talk about that.

But any objections she had dissolved the moment she stepped into the foyer. The scent wrapped around her, and with it came something else—a feeling of profound homecoming that made her heart swell with emotion.

Pocket doors off the foyer opened into a grand living room with soaring ceilings and tall windows that flooded the space with light. A massive stone fireplace dominated one wall, its mantel carved with intricate maritime motifs—

anchors, ship wheels, and what appeared to be lighthouse beams radiating outward. Built-in bookcases flanked the hearth, their shelves empty, as if they'd been waiting decades for the right books to fill them.

But something odd struck her. They weren't entirely empty—a single volume sat spine-out on the middle shelf, its leather binding worn smooth. *Maritime Disasters of the Maine Coast, 1850-1875*. Fresh fingerprints marred the dusty cover, as if someone had recently pulled it out and hastily replaced it.

Nora moved slowly through the space, her sneakers making no sound on the gleaming hardwood floors. The wide planks were original, worn smooth by generations of footsteps but still glowing with warm honey tones. Crown molding traced elegant lines where walls met the ceiling, and every window was framed by interior shutters that had been painted and repainted so many times their surfaces had the soft, undulating texture of driftwood.

It was beautiful. Beyond beautiful, it was perfect—exactly what she'd pictured when she'd made the impulsive decision to buy the house sight unseen and leave behind her cramped Manhattan apartment and the endless cycle of commercial work that had been slowly killing her creative spirit.

But there was something else, something that made her pulse quicken. Standing in the soft light of this room with its lingering scent of vanilla and cinnamon, she felt … home. For the first time in years, maybe for the first time ever, she felt like she'd found the place where she belonged.

She moved from room to room like someone in a dream. The dining room held a beautiful built-in china cabinet, its glass doors reflecting the afternoon light in prismatic rainbows. The study was lined with empty bookshelves and featured a window seat that looked like the perfect spot for reading on rainy days. Everything was exactly as Milt had promised—freshly painted, polished, and gleaming—ready for her new life.

The kitchen drew her like a magnet. She'd seen it in the listing photos, of course—a spacious room with white cabinets, butcher block countertops, and a farmhouse sink positioned beneath a window that looked out at a sweeping back lawn. But the photos hadn't captured the way the afternoon light from that window cast everything in a warm hue.

As she moved deeper into the house, she began to notice things that weren't exactly as Milt had described in his last update—paint cans stacked in corners, drop cloths draped over furniture, and the faint smell of fresh paint.

A floorboard creaked overhead—a long, deliberate sound, like someone shifting their weight. Nora froze, listening. Old houses settled, she reminded herself. But this hadn't sounded like settling. This sounded like footsteps.

Her phone buzzed in her pocket just as she reached the kitchen at the back of the house. The caller ID made her smile: *Milt Thurlow, Coastal Carpentry.*

"Hey, Milt," she answered, pressing the phone to her ear as she took in the spacious room.

"Nora! You made it safe and sound, I hope?" His gravelly voice carried the warm Down East accent she'd grown fond of during their phone conversations over the past several months.

"I just walked through the front door," she said, moving to the front of the house to gaze out at the harbor. "Milt, the house is gorgeous, but I'm seeing some paint supplies."

"Ah, about that." She could hear a sheepish tone creeping into his voice. "I meant to call you before you left the city. We hit a little snag with the upstairs bathroom—old pipes, you know how it is. Had to tear into the wall more than we expected. We're about ninety percent done, but I didn't want to rush the finishing work and have it look shoddy."

Nora leaned against the counter, surprised by how little this news bothered her. A month ago, any deviation from her meticulous plans would have sent her into a spiral of anxiety. "How long are we talking?"

"Another week, maybe ten days? I've got my best guys on it, Danny and Rick. You'll meet them tomorrow. They're good guys, neat workers. They won't be in your way too much." He paused. "I know this isn't what you wanted to hear on your first day …"

"It's fine, Milt, really." And it was fine. As she watched the changing light on the harbor, she felt a sense of peace that wouldn't be disturbed by a few workers finishing up renovations. "As long as I have a working bathroom downstairs and the kitchen is functional."

"Ayuh, everything downstairs is shipshape. The kitchen's been done for days. We installed new appliances yesterday, in fact. You've got everything you need." His relief was audible. "I left some basic supplies in the pantry, too. Coffee, bread, and a couple of frozen dinners in the freezer. I figured you might not want to venture out on your first night."

"You're amazing, Milt. Thank you." Nora paused, then added, "Oh, and I love whatever scent system you installed. The whole house smells like vanilla and cinnamon—it's so welcoming."

There was a brief silence on the other end. "Scent system? I didn't install anything like that, Nora. Must be something the previous owners left behind. Or maybe it's just the old wood and whatever the cleaning crew used."

"Huh." Nora glanced around the foyer, inhaling the sweet, spiced air. "Well, whatever it is, it's lovely."

"Ayuh, old houses have their own personalities," Milt said with a chuckle. "Sometimes they hold on to smells for decades. My grandmother's house still smells like her apple pies, and she's been gone twenty years."

"Now, about heat—the furnace is running, but I've noticed that some of those upstairs rooms get chilly. I left some space heaters in the hall closet if you need them. We can talk about adding some heat to the upstairs if you want."

They talked for a few more minutes about practical details—where to find the circuit breakers, which local restaurants delivered, and the best grocery store in town. When they hung up, Nora felt even more settled about her decision to buy the house. Milt's fatherly concern reminded her why she'd trusted him to oversee the renovations from five hundred miles away.

She was still standing at the kitchen sink, admiring the view, when she remembered she'd promised to call Caroline once she arrived. Her best friend had been sending increasingly frantic texts all day.

Caroline picked up on the first ring. "Please tell me you haven't been murdered by some creepy Maine hermit and this is actually your ghost calling me."

"How did you know?" Nora laughed, settling into one of the two folding chairs Milt had left around a small table. "I'm very much alive and currently sitting in my beautiful new house looking out at the harbor."

"Thank God. I've been spiraling all day thinking about you driving up there alone to a house you've never seen." Caroline's voice carried a blend of affection and exasperation. "So? Don't keep me in suspense. Is it horrible? Please tell me it's not some decrepit Victorian nightmare with bats in the attic."

A door upstairs clicked shut—soft but distinct.

Nora glanced up, then stood. "It's perfect," she said, higher-pitched than intended. She moved toward the staircase, peering up into the darkness. "Better than the photos, actually. The light in here is incredible, and the harbor view …" She trailed off as she turned to watch a sailboat glide across the rippling water. "I can already see about six paintings I want to start."

"That's my girl. And the contractor situation? Last I heard, he was supposed to be finished by now."

Nora filled her in on her conversation with Milt—the delayed bathroom work, the supplies he'd left, and his promise that the workers would stay out of her way. "Honestly, I think I prefer it this way. It gives me time to settle in gradually instead of trying to make everything perfect all at once."

"Wow, this is not the Nora I knew during your apartment renovation," Caroline observed. "I seem to recall when your kitchen contractor was three days late, and you called me crying at midnight."

The comparison struck Nora. Six months ago, even three days behind schedule would have sent her into a panic. Now, the idea of having workers around while she settled into her new life seemed almost cozy. "I guess I'm more relaxed now."

"I can hear it in your voice—you sound more relaxed than you have in years." Caroline paused. "I'm proud of you, you know. For taking this leap."

"Even though you thought I was crazy for buying a house sight unseen?"

"*Especially* because I thought you were crazy for buying a house sight unseen. You've been playing it safe for so long, Nora. This is precisely the kind of beautiful, impulsive decision you needed to make."

They talked for another ten minutes—Caroline updating

her on art gallery gossip, Nora describing the house room by room. When they hung up, the afternoon light had begun to deepen toward evening.

While she looked through the pantry and fridge at what Milt had left her, absorbed in planning the paintings she would create, she became aware of a sound—soft, rhythmic, like someone gently tapping fingers on wood. It seemed to come from everywhere and nowhere at once.

Then, a thud behind her made her jump.

Nora turned, her heart beating faster. There on the kitchen floor beside the island lay a wooden rolling pin. It was beautiful—old and worn, the kind of utensil that spoke of decades of loving use. She didn't recall having seen it minutes before.

She approached it cautiously, as if it might disappear if she moved too quickly. When she knelt to pick it up, she saw initials carved into the handle: "M.W."

The wood was warm beneath her fingers, warmer than it should have been after lying untouched in an empty kitchen. As she turned it over in her hands, the scent of vanilla and cinnamon grew more intense, as if swirling around her.

It's an old house, she told herself firmly, setting the rolling pin carefully on the counter. Old houses settle. The floors can't be perfectly level after all these years. Things shift.

She continued exploring the house. Upstairs, she found four bedrooms, each with its own character and charm. The master bedroom faced the harbor, with French doors that opened onto a small balcony. Standing there, she could imagine waking up to the sight of the sunrise over the water, a cup of coffee in hand, or watching the fishing boats head out for their morning runs.

But it was the bedroom beside it, also facing the harbor,

that called to her most. The moment she stepped inside, she knew this would be her studio. The spacious room had multiple windows on the front and east sides, with the front offering views of the ocean. The slanted ceiling gave the room a cozy, intimate feeling despite its generous size.

On the windowsill sat a delicate teacup, half-full of liquid that hadn't quite evaporated. The faint scent of chamomile lingered in the air. Nora wondered about it, then decided it must have been left by one of the workers—a cleaner, perhaps.

Best of all, the lighting was perfect for painting. There was enough space for her easel, supply cabinets, and canvases. If needed, she could use the back bedroom for storage.

Standing in this room filled her with the same sense of rightness she'd felt in the kitchen, as if the room had been waiting, patient and hopeful, for someone to fill it with creative passion once more.

By the time she'd finished her exploration, the afternoon light had begun to fade. Nora retrieved her single suitcase from the Mini Cooper, along with the air mattress and bedding she'd brought for her first night.

She set up the air mattress in the master bedroom, arranging her pillows and blankets until she had a cozy nest beside the French doors. From here, she could watch the changing light on the harbor and fall asleep to the sound of waves crashing against the rocky shore.

There was just one thing missing. She headed downstairs, where the bottle of wine she'd brought sat on the counter. This seemed like the perfect time to open it. She smiled as she discovered a pair of wine glasses in one of the kitchen cabinets. They were modern. She smiled. Milt must have left them for her along with the groceries. Nora poured herself a generous serving.

She carried the glass to the front windows and stood watching as the sun sank toward the horizon, painting the harbor in shades of gold and crimson that she hoped she might one day capture on canvas.

This was what she'd come here for—the peaceful sense of knowing she was where she was meant to be. For years, she'd felt like she was living someone else's life, painting someone else's vision of beauty and charm. But here, in this house that already felt like home, she could feel her true artistic spirit stirring to life.

The light continued to change as the warm afternoon light gave way to the deeper hues of early evening. Brooding clouds gathered on the horizon, promising the kind of weather that made artists reach for their brushes. In the twilight, the harbor took on a mysterious quality as shadows lengthened and the first lights began to twinkle in the windows of houses along the shoreline.

She was halfway back to the kitchen to refill her glass when she heard a car door slam, followed by the measured sound of footsteps on the wooden porch steps.

Milt? She set her glass on the counter and headed down the long, oak-paneled hall to the front door. She'd told him she didn't need him to check on her tonight, but maybe he decided to stop by anyway. Or it could be the moving company. But if there had been a scheduling change, they should have called her. She heaved a sigh. Moving furniture in as the sun set would not have been her first choice.

The knock came just as she reached the foyer—a firm, confident sound that echoed through the empty house. Nora smoothed her hair, suddenly aware that she probably looked like she'd been driving for eight hours, which she had, and pulled open the heavy oak door.

The man standing on her porch was definitely not from a moving company.

He was tall—about six feet two inches—with broad shoulders that filled out a cream-colored Irish knit sweater to perfection. Dark hair caught the porch light, a bit tousled, and when he looked up from the antique pocket watch in his palm, she was met with eyes the color of storm clouds gathering over the ocean. His face was ruggedly handsome in a way that spoke of Maine winters and salt air, with strong cheekbones and jawline, an overall look that suggested he was no stranger to hard work. But it was his hands that caught her attention. Strong and well-formed, they were the kind of hands that could handle a fishing line or turn the pages of a book with equal ease.

"I'm sorry to bother you," he said, with just a hint of a Down East accent that charmed her. "But I believe this came from your house."

Nora stared at him, then at the watch, then back at his face. The watch in his palm was old, its gold case tarnished with age, and even from where she stood, she could hear it ticking with a steady, purposeful beat.

The moment stretched between them, silent except for the rhythmic ticking. There was something about this man —the way he held himself, the intensity in those storm-gray eyes—that commanded attention, not in an aggressive way, but with the quiet confidence of someone accustomed to being taken seriously.

"I …" she began, then stopped, collecting her thoughts. Whatever this was about, it felt important. "I'm sorry, but I don't understand."

He smiled—a slow expression that transformed his entire face from merely handsome to compelling, devastatingly so.

"I'm Maddox Hale," he said, stepping closer, "and I think you and I need to talk."

CHAPTER TWO

THREE DAYS Earlier

Maddox Hale sat at the scarred oak desk in his family's seaside cottage, staring at the email that had arrived at 9:47 a.m. and effectively ended his academic career. The message from Hartwell University Press was brief and devastatingly courteous:

> *Dear Dr. Hale,*
>
> *After careful consideration, we must decline to publish "Shipwrecked: The Untold Story of Maine's Most Enigmatic Maritime Tragedies." While your passion for the subject is evident, the manuscript relies too heavily on family anecdotes and unsubstantiated folklore. We feel the work would benefit from a more scholarly, evidence-based approach before it could meet our publication standards.*
>
> *We wish you the best in your future endeavors.*
> *Sincerely,*
> *Rachel Davenport, PhD*
> *Senior Editor*

Unsubstantiated folklore. The phrase had been echoing in his head for hours, each repetition feeling like another nail in the coffin of everything he'd worked toward for the past five years.

Maddox had always prided himself on being a rational man. Even when his academic colleagues whispered that he was too emotionally invested in his research, even when his family rolled their eyes at another dinner conversation about maritime history, he'd maintained that his pursuit of the truth about his great-great-grandfather was grounded in solid scholarship and documented facts.

Today, however, rational thought seemed to have abandoned him entirely.

This had been his last chance. After Rockland declined to renew his teaching contract—officially due to "budget constraints," though everyone knew it was really because his obsession with one particular maritime tragedy had begun to eclipse his other scholarly work—Hartwell had been the only academic publisher willing to even consider his manuscript.

Now that door had slammed shut, too.

He poured himself three fingers of Talisker—a bottle he'd been saving for the day his book got accepted—and was contemplating the bitter irony when his gaze fell on the FedEx box that had been delivered earlier. He'd seen Miranda's return address and set it aside, too focused on the publisher's rejection to deal with whatever fresh hell that represented.

But with his academic career now in ruins, curiosity won out over self-preservation.

Inside, he found the remnants of their year-long relationship, packed with a bitter efficiency that spoke volumes. Research materials—mostly maritime history books that had been scattered around her apartment—

photocopied ship manifests and lighthouse records that had been cluttering his nightstand, and even a folder of his notes on 19th-century weather patterns. She'd wanted every trace of his obsession out of her space.

His clothes were there too, stuffed in as packing material with obvious haste. A few sweaters, the electric toothbrush from her bathroom counter, and that bottle of cologne she'd bought him for his birthday, still in its original packaging. He'd worn it once, the night she'd given it to him. Inexplicably, he found a single navy-blue sock crumpled and covered in dust, as if she'd been so eager to purge him from her life that she'd thrown in whatever random item she'd found in the closet corners.

But it was the small bundle wrapped in tissue paper that made his chest tighten with recognition. He unwrapped it, already knowing what he'd find: the broken pieces of his favorite coffee mug. It had been nothing fancy —white ceramic with a simple maritime compass design— but he'd used it every morning for two years. It had become part of his routine, as essential as his first cup of coffee.

Now it was just ceramic shards, packaged with vindictive care. She'd probably thrown it at the wall after their last fight, then decided to send him the pieces because she was thorough like that. *Oh, you want your stuff? Here it is! All of it. Every. Last. Bit.*

A note was tucked between the research folders, written in her precise handwriting:

> *Maddox,*
> *I came across some more stuff of yours. Here you go.*
> *I hope you find what you're looking for. I just know it's not me.*
> *Miranda*

*P.S. — I'm keeping the espresso maker. You never used it
anyway.*

Buried beneath the research papers was something he'd
forgotten he'd even brought to her apartment: a small
scrimshaw box that had belonged to his great-great-grandfather Elias. The whalebone surface was intricately carved
with maritime scenes—ships navigating stormy seas, a
lighthouse beam cutting through darkness—and "E.W."
was etched in elegant script on the lid. Miranda had
admired it once, and he'd offhandedly mentioned that it
contained some family mementos—nothing valuable, just
sentimental pieces that his grandmother had saved. Now
she'd clearly packed it with the rest of his research as one
more piece of his past that she wanted out of her present.

But how could he explain that Elias Wheeler's story
wasn't just family history to him? How could he make her
understand that clearing his great-great-grandfather's
name felt like clearing his own?

The official records painted Elias as a reckless captain
who'd taken unnecessary risks in a storm and paid the ulti-
mate price. But Maddox had found inconsistencies in the
lighthouse keeper's logs, discrepancies in the weather
reports, and hints that there was more to the story than
anyone had bothered to investigate. Elias had been a skilled
mariner, cautious and experienced. The idea that he'd sail
into a known storm made no sense.

Just like the idea that Maddox was "too emotionally
invested" made no sense to him. How else should a historian approach the truth? With cold detachment? With scholarly distance that stripped away the human cost of tragedy?

The third and final blow had come at 6:15 p.m., in the
form of a voicemail from his mother that he'd played three
times, each listening more painful than the last:

"Maddox, darling, I just heard the most wonderful news! Miranda is engaged to that lovely cardiologist she met at her sister's wedding—you remember Dr. Phillips, don't you? Such a nice man, and he actually shows up at her family gatherings. He's charming and doesn't spend every conversation talking about dead relatives." A pause, during which he could practically hear her steeling herself for the kill shot. "I suppose I've given up hope of grandchildren at this point. Your father and I have been more than patient with this ... obsession of yours, but we can't support you indefinitely. Perhaps it's time to consider a more practical career path. I'm sure your great-great-grandfather's ghost will keep you company in your old age, but the rest of us are getting tired of waiting for you to rejoin the living. Call me when you're ready to discuss your future realistically."

Maddox stared at his phone long after the message ended, feeling the weight of utter failure settle upon him. His academic career was in ruins, his relationship was over, and his family's patience had ended. Here he was, thirty-four years old, with no prospects, no income, and a manuscript that no one took seriously.

He poured himself a drink and settled into the leather chair by the window that overlooked Mariner's Bluff harbor. The irony wasn't lost on him. Here he sat, drowning his sorrows while staring out at the very waters that had claimed Elias's life 150 years ago.

Maybe everyone was right. Maybe he was chasing ghosts. Maybe it was time to give up, pack away his research, and figure out what the hell else he was qualified to do with his life.

The Scotch burned warm in his chest as he contemplated his options. He could probably get a job teaching high school history—if he was lucky. Maybe work at the maritime museum giving tours to tourists who were more interested in gift shop souvenirs than actual history. The thought made him physically ill.

The combination of alcohol, exhaustion, and emotional devastation finally overtook him. His eyes grew heavy as he stared out at the darkening harbor, and before he knew it, he'd drifted off in the chair.

RAIN LASHES HIS FACE, and wind howls around him. He stands on the deck of a ship, but he is not himself—he is someone else, someone desperate to reach home. The harbor lies ahead, and his eyes search frantically for the lighthouse beam that should guide him safely to port. There—he can see the light sweeping across the water, steady and reassuring. But then, impossibly, it goes out. Complete darkness, where the beacon should be, left him blind in the storm.

MADDOX JOLTED AWAKE, his heart pounding. The dream had felt so real he could still taste salt spray on his lips. He sat disoriented for a moment, the phantom sensation of a ship's deck rolling beneath his feet slowly fading.

Just a dream. Too much research, too much scotch, and too much emotional upheaval for one day. His mind was playing tricks on him, weaving together all the maritime history he'd been studying into some kind of vivid nightmare.

He was reaching for the bottle to pour himself another drink to steady his nerves when his gaze fell on the cardboard box Miranda had sent back. The research materials were scattered where he'd pulled them out, but tucked beneath a folder of lighthouse records was something he hadn't noticed before.

Curious now, and perhaps motivated by the scotch and the need for some connection to better times, he pulled his great-grandmother's scrimshaw box from beside his chair and set it on the small deck table. The hinges resisted with a soft squeak as he lifted the lid, revealing the collection of items he hadn't looked at in years: his great-grandmother's wedding ring, a few old photographs, and an ornate hat pin that had belonged to some long-dead relative.

And there, nestled in the corner beneath a faded ribbon, was Elias's pocket watch.

Maddox lifted it carefully from the chest, surprised by how solid it felt in his palm. He'd seen it countless times as a child—his grandmother used to let him hold it while she told stories about the family's seafaring past. But it had been just that: a broken keepsake, a conversation piece that hadn't ticked in living memory.

The gold case was tarnished with age, its surface elaborately engraved with maritime motifs that caught the last of the evening light: anchors, ship wheels, and what looked like lighthouse beams radiating outward in intricate detail. The craftsmanship was exquisite, clearly the work of a master jeweler from an era when such things were built to last.

Maddox turned it over in his hands, remembering his grandmother's stories. The watch had stopped the day Elias died, she'd always said. No watchmaker had ever been able to repair it, though several had tried over the decades. It had become a symbol of sorts—time stopped, a life cut short, a story left unfinished.

Last week, he'd been walking through town, following a lead about properties that Elias had owned or might have visited. The trail led him to the Captain's Watch, the Victorian mansion on Mariner's Bluff that had recently been sold to an artist from New York. He stopped by on the off chance that the new owner might let him examine the house for any historical connections to his great-great-grandfather.

A CONTRACTOR'S truck was parked in the driveway. Thurlow Construction. He knew Milt, a gruff but friendly man who was happy to talk about the house's history while he worked on some final renovation details.

"Elias Wheeler, you say?" Milt scratched his gray head thoughtfully. "Can't say I know the name, but this house has been home to a lot of seafaring families over the years. Built in 1869, so the timing would be about right."

They'd talked for close to an hour—about the house's architecture, its various owners, and the way maritime families had shaped the character of Mariner's Bluff. Maddox had mentioned his research, and Milt had seemed interested, even offering to put him in touch with the new owner when she arrived.

"Nice lady, from what I've gathered in phone conversations," Milt said. "An artist specializing in maritime scenes. She might appreciate talking to someone who knows the history of these waters. She's supposed to arrive this coming Tuesday."

Maddox had left his contact information and thought nothing more of it. But as he walked back to his car, a sound drew his attention. Not the hesitant, struggling tick of an old mechanism trying to come back to life, but a strong, steady, purposeful beat. Maddox pulled the pocket watch out and stared at it in shock. That couldn't be. Maybe it was the stress, the complete upending of his life, that was causing his mind to play tricks on him.

But the ticking continued, clear and insistent.

THREE DAYS Later

As Maddox peered at the now silent watch in his hand, he believed in his soul that the watch had been ticking at the Captain's Watch. He wasn't losing his mind. He couldn't be. But he had to know. He had to be certain.

The new owner had arrived today, according to Milt's timeline. Which meant she was there now, in the house where this watch had suddenly, impossibly, come back to life.

Maddox grabbed his windbreaker from the back of a chair and slipped the watch into his pocket. He didn't know what he was going to say to the owner. There was no way to explain what was happening without sounding like a complete lunatic.

But he knew, with the kind of bone-deep certainty that had nothing to do with rational thought, that everything in his life had led to this moment. The failed career, the ended relationship, the family's disapproval—all of it had been leading him here, to this house, to this woman, to whatever truth was waiting to be uncovered.

The walk from his cottage to the Captain's Watch took fifteen minutes, but as he drew closer, the watch began ticking, growing stronger with each step. By the time he reached the front gate, it was practically vibrating in his palm, as if it recognized home.

Light spilled from the windows of the Victorian mansion, and he could see a figure moving around inside—

a woman with dark hair who moved with fluid grace. The new owner. The artist.

The woman who somehow held the key to everything he'd been searching for.

Maddox climbed the porch steps, his heart hammering in rhythm with the pocket watch's urgent ticking. This was either the moment when his research would finally be vindicated or the moment when he'd prove once and for all that everyone was right about him being obsessed and delusional.

He raised his hand to knock on the ornate oak door, and the watch seemed to tick louder, as if approving of his decision.

Whatever happened next, there was no turning back.

CHAPTER THREE

THE MAN STANDING on her porch was not from a moving company.

Nora had been expecting Milt's nephew Danny to drop off the new bathroom fixtures or maybe one of the other workmen who'd forgotten a tool. Instead, she stood face-to-face with a tall, broad-shouldered stranger in jeans and a cable-knit sweater who looked like he'd stepped out of the mist rolling in from the harbor—attractive in a way that made her forget she was wearing old sweats and a worn-out t-shirt.

His gray eyes met hers with an intensity that made her heart skip a beat. He extended his hand. "I'm Maddox Hale, and I think you and I need to talk."

Before she could ask what that was supposed to mean, the sound of rushing water and cursing rang out from the kitchen. From the sound of it, Milt's day had just gotten worse.

"Nora Delaney." With a backward glance toward the kitchen, she shook his hand. "Would you excuse me for a minute?"

"Nora!" Milt called out from the kitchen, his voice tinged with urgency. "We've got a situation here!"

"On my way." She glanced back at Maddox Hale and continued to the kitchen, torn between curiosity about her unexpected visitor and whatever was going on in the kitchen. As she walked away, she glanced down and caught sight of her stained t-shirt and winced.

"Milt? I thought the kitchen was finished."

He gave the pipe under the sink one more twist of his wrench, then turned around and glared. "A house this old is never finished."

She stared at the puddle of water spreading across the floor from the sink. "What happened?"

"The pipe joint gave way," he explained, getting up from his battle with the rebellious plumbing. With a wave of his hand, he said, "Hand me that mop."

Nora grabbed the mop while Milt rose to his feet. As he mopped up the floor, he said, "Nothing major, but it's made a hell of a mess."

"Can I do anything?"

"No, I'll call Danny. I'll have to shut off the water for the night."

Nora took a moment to process the idea of a night with no water.

Seeing her dismay, Milt added, "Just in the kitchen. I'd fix it now, but I don't have the parts."

"Oh, okay." She glanced toward the hallway. "I left somebody at the front door. So ..." She started to walk away but turned back. "Milt?"

Milt propped the mop up against the wall and turned to Nora while wiping his hands with a rag. "It's just a joint. I'll replace it in the morning and have you back up and running by noon."

"Okay." She stepped closer and lowered her voice. "Milt, do you know a Maddox Hale?"

"Yeah, what about him?"

She whispered, "He's at my front door."

Nora tried to stop him, but he took a few steps to the doorway, looked down the hallway, and waved. "Maddox! How's it going?"

Maddox waved back. "Hi, Milt. Good."

Milt turned away and started packing up his tools. "He's okay. Not an axe murderer, if that's what you're thinking."

"Well, no, not exactly. I just …"

Milt looked up from his toolbox and waited.

"Never mind." With a gesture toward the door, she said, "I should …"

Milt closed his toolbox. "Oh, and don't mind me." Then he lowered his voice. "I'm not an axe murderer either." He chuckled and walked out the door.

Nora sighed and headed back down the hall to the door, where Maddox was still waiting.

"I'm sorry. I just moved in—today, actually. And things are kind of a mess."

"I know."

Alarmed, Nora shot back, "You know?"

He held up a hand as if that would assuage her concern. "I stopped by yesterday, and Milt told me you'd be here."

In her mind, Nora replayed Milt's assurance that Maddox was okay. *He's not an axe murderer. He's not an axe murderer.*

"This might sound kind of strange," Maddox hesitated. "But there's a connection between this house and my family history. My great-great-grandfather lived in the Captain's Watch in the 1870s, and this pocket watch belonged to him."

He pulled an antique watch from his jacket pocket, and Nora took in the elaborate maritime engravings on its tarnished gold case. "It's beautiful. Oh, and it still works."

Maddox's eyebrows drew together as he studied the watch. "Yes ... about that ..."

The watch ticked so loudly it couldn't be ignored. Nor could the silence between them that followed.

Seeing Maddox's fixation on the ticking watch, Nora tried not to sound condescending. "It's what watches do. Tick. Right? The old ones, anyway."

As if coming out of a trance, Maddox looked up at her. "Not this one. It's been broken for as long as I've owned it." His eyes fixed on hers intently. "The thing is, it did the same thing yesterday when I was here talking to Milt."

That did seem a little unusual, Nora had to admit. "Maybe there's some sort of magnetic field here or something."

Maddox echoed distractedly, "Or something."

"So, Mr. Hale, what brings you here?"

"I'm researching a shipwreck."

Nora glanced past Maddox to the harbor. While the view was spectacular, it was far enough away that she couldn't make the connection to her house.

Maddox followed her gaze to the water. "A ship wrecked out there in 1871, and its captain, Elias Wheeler, went down with the ship. He was my great-great-grandfather, and this was his house."

"That's interesting." She suppressed a yawn. "I'm sorry. It's been a very long day. I drove eight hours to get here. Could we talk another time?"

"Yes, of course." He reached into his satchel and pulled out a springback binder. "Why don't I leave this with you? It's a book I've been writing about the shipwreck. It explains why I'm here."

Nora took the manuscript, opened it to the first page, and read: *Shipwrecked: The Untold Story of One of Maine's Most Enigmatic Maritime Tragedies* by Dr. Maddox Hale. The watch's loud ticking continued.

Maddox slipped the watch back into his pocket. "Please take a look, if you would. I'll be in touch."

Without thinking, Nora agreed.

The smile Maddox returned was worth the promise. "Thank you."

She watched him walk to his car and then looked at the manuscript in her hands.

BY NINE O'CLOCK, Nora set a moving box back down and decided to tackle it in the morning. The house felt strange with only overhead room lights and dark, curtainless windows. That was to be expected, she reminded herself. It was her first night, and the furniture hadn't arrived. But soon, she'd be unpacked and settled, and it would feel like the comfortable home she'd imagined.

She headed upstairs to her studio. The day's chaos had left her restless, craving the peace that only this room seemed to provide. Tonight the view was spectacular—a full moon hanging low over the harbor, its light painting everything in silver and shadow. Clouds drifted across the sky, and the distant lighthouse swept its beam in a steady, hypnotic rhythm.

She poured herself a generous glass of wine, settled into the folding wood and canvas beach chair she'd positioned by the window, and picked up Maddox's manuscript. It had been years since she'd read anything by an academic, so she braced herself for a dry maritime history.

October 3, 1871

The wind that had been nothing more than a whisper at dawn now howled across harbor like something alive and hungry. In the house on Mariner's Bluff, Mabel Wheeler pressed her hand to the slight swell of her belly and watched the harbor through rain-lashed windows, counting the days until her husband's return.

October 3, 1871

Twenty miles offshore, Captain Elias Wheeler stood on the deck of the merchant vessel Steadfast and studied the darkening sky with the eye of a man who had sailed these waters for fifteen years. The barometer had been falling steadily since noon, and the wind that had started as a favorable breeze now carried the metallic taste of a nor'easter building to the south.

A younger captain might have put into port, content to wait out the storm in safe harbor. But Elias carried more than cargo in his hold—he carried the hopes of an entire community preparing for winter, and more than that, he carried the eager heart of a man desperate to be home with his wife.

Three months at sea felt like three years when you were newly married and deeply in love.

From his jacket pocket, he pulled a letter worn soft from handling—Mabel's last correspondence, received when the Steadfast had docked briefly in Boston. Her elegant script covered both sides of the paper with news of the garden she was planting, the curtains she was sewing for their bedroom, and the warmth of the morning sun pouring in through the kitchen window while she took her breakfast each day. But it was the final paragraph that he returned to again and again.

I have such wonderful news to share. It feels too precious to trust to paper, and yet I can't wait. Our family is soon to be three. I dream of tiny hands and eyes that have your storm-gray color. Come home soon.

Elias smiled despite the worsening weather. His Mabel's talk of dreams filled him with such fierce joy that he nearly laughed aloud. A child. Their child. The future they had dreamed of in whispered conversations as they lay entwined was now coming true.

No storm would keep him from that future.

"Mr. Banks!" he called to his first mate, who was securing the rigging with methodical care. "What do you make of the weather?"

Emerson Banks had sailed with Elias for seven years and trusted his captain's judgment above his own. But as he studied the roiling clouds building on the horizon, he felt the familiar tightness in his chest that came before bad weather.

"Storm's moving fast, Captain. Faster than I'd like. We could put into Portsmouth and wait it out."

Elias considered this. Portsmouth meant safety, but it also meant delay—possibly days if the storm proved as fierce as it appeared. Days away from Mabel.

"How long to Mariner's Harbor?"

"Two hours if the wind holds steady. Three if it worsens."

Three hours. Elias looked again at the lighthouse beam cutting through the gathering dusk, steady and sure as it had been every night for twelve years. Jasper Shaw, the lighthouse keeper, was as reliable as sunrise. The light would guide them into port well before the storm worsened.

"We make for home, Mr. Banks. The Steadfast has seen worse weather than this."

The Steadfast struck Gull's Rest at 10:23 p.m. with an impact that would have sent men sprawling across the deck. He might have struggled to his feet, but the ship would have shuddered beneath him and broken apart.

Mabel jolted awake from an uneasy sleep. Her hand flew to her throat as if hearing a cry. The storm was at its peak now. She rushed to the window and looked into the darkness. The sweeping beam of the lighthouse was dark.

She pressed her face to the glass, straining to see through the rain and wind. Something was wrong. She could feel it.

"Come home," she whispered to the darkness. "Please, my love, come home."

But Elias Wheeler would never come home again.

Survivors testified that the lighthouse beam had gone out, but their reports were unsubstantiated. Upon careful inspection, the light was in perfect order with no evidence of malfunction. The official inquiry, completed two months later, concluded that Captain Wheeler had shown poor judgment in attempting to make port during dangerous weather conditions.

Mabel Wheeler, who had been known for her robust health and high spirits, began to fade almost immediately after her husband's death, growing paler and more fragile with each passing day.

The whispers started within a week of the Steadfast's loss. Seven men dead because Captain Wheeler had been too reckless, too eager to reach home to wait out the storm safely. Some said he'd been drinking. Others suggested that, at the young age of thirty-one, he was overconfident and careless. The kindest voices merely called it poor judgment, a moment's miscalculation that had cost too much.

Mabel heard every word murmured in the market, whispered at church, and even directly from well-meaning neighbors who thought she should know the "truth" about her husband's final voyage. Each cruel assessment of Elias's character struck her like a harsh blow until she could barely leave the house without feeling the community's judgment.

When Mrs. Hartwell cornered her outside the general store and said, with false sympathy, "At least you won't have to worry about him leaving you again, dear. Perhaps this was God's way of teaching him the cost of selfishness." Something inside Mabel simply … broke.

The child she carried lived only as long as her hope did. When the last piece of wreckage from the Steadfast washed ashore—a piece of the ship's wheel that Elias had carved with their initials—Mabel's body finally acknowledged what her heart had known from the moment the lighthouse went dark.

She miscarried on October 28th, exactly twenty-five days after losing her husband.

Three days later, on Halloween night, Mabel Wheeler died in her sleep. She was buried beside the husband she had loved for six months.

Questions remained, waiting in the shadows of the official record, refusing to be silenced.

NORA SET down the manuscript with a sigh. "How desperately tragic."

As she spoke, a sudden chill filled the room. She set down the pages and looked around the studio with the oddest feeling she wasn't alone. The moonlight streaming through the windows had taken on an ethereal quality, and the shadows in the corners of the room seemed deeper.

She stood and went to the window where the lights shimmered in the harbor and headlights lit the road, guiding cars on their way.

Nora exhaled. "Well, now you're just being silly."

With a shiver, she left the studio for the warmth of her bedroom, making a mental note to ask Milt about heating.

CHAPTER FOUR

For the first time since arriving in Maine, Nora woke to the luxurious sound of silence after days of chaos and power tools echoing through the house. She stretched in her own bed, in her own room, marveling at how different everything felt. The furniture delivery and subsequent unpacking marathon were behind her now, and after a week of settling in, the Captain's Watch finally felt like home.

She padded downstairs in her pajamas and fuzzy slippers, marveling at how the house had transformed. Her paintings—the real ones, not the commercial work—hung on the walls where the morning light could catch them properly. A large sketchpad stood ready by the living room's tall windows, positioned to capture the harbor view that had drawn her here in the first place.

As she made her morning coffee, the vanilla-cinnamon scent seemed stronger. She settled into the window seat with her mug, looking out at the harbor, where fishing boats were already heading out for their morning runs.

Maddox's manuscript lay on the coffee table, where

she'd left it. She'd read it twice now, each time more moved
by the tragic love story. As she flipped through the pages
again, her artist's mind began forming images. She could
picture the *Steadfast* fighting through the storm and could
see Elias at the helm, with his wife's letter clutched in his
weathered hand.

Without thinking about it, she reached for her sketchpad
and began drawing. The *Steadfast* took shape beneath her
fingers—a merchant vessel struggling against towering
waves, its sails straining against the wind. She focused on
the details that made the story feel real: the way the rigging
would look in a storm, the angle of the ship as it fought the
waves, and the lighthouse beam cutting through the
darkness.

When she looked up from the page, her coffee had gone
cold, and the harbor was bright with the full morning sun.
She'd been drawing for over an hour, lost in the scene that
had played out in her mind.

A knock at the front door interrupted her thoughts.
Through the window, she saw Maddox on the porch. She
glanced down at her pajamas—soft cotton pants covered in
tiny sailboats and a tank top that had seen better days—and
decided she was past caring about appearances.

"Good morning," she said as she opened the door,
suddenly aware of how her voice sounded rougher than
usual.

"Hello." His eyes crinkled at the corners as he took in
her pajamas, and she caught that hint of sea salt and cedar
that seemed to follow him. "I hope you don't mind my
stopping by. I wanted to pick up my manuscript, but I was
also hoping you might have a few minutes to talk." He
trailed off, running a hand through his dark hair.

"Come in." She stepped aside, gesturing toward the
living room. "Would you like some coffee?"

"That sounds perfect."

As she led him toward the kitchen, she said, "I made it a while ago, so no promises. How do you take it?"

"Black, thanks."

She poured him a mug and refilled her own, acutely aware of his presence in her kitchen. He was wearing jeans and a forest green sweatshirt, and she wondered if there was anything he didn't look good in.

"Your manuscript," she began as they walked back to the living room, "is beautiful. Heartbreaking, but beautiful."

"Thanks." There was something vulnerable in his voice.

"The story's so tragic, but compelling." She handed him the manuscript, their fingers brushing for just a moment. "I can see why it means so much to you."

"I was hoping …" He stopped, glancing around the room. "This house has such history, and they lived here. So I thought it might contain a clue that could help with my research."

Something in his tone roused her suspicion. "What sort of clue?" she asked.

The moment stretched between them. His posture shifted, and when he spoke again, his voice was lighter. "I'm sorry. I'm being presumptuous. It's just—I've reached a point in my research where I'm kind of stuck." He averted his eyes and caught sight of her sketchpad on the coffee table. "Milt said you're an artist."

Grateful for the change of subject, she nodded. "That's actually why I moved here. I've been painting commercial work for years, but I needed a change." She gestured toward the harbor view. "That's where my heart is—the coast, the ocean, the boats. I've always been drawn to maritime scenes."

Maddox moved closer to look at her sketch, and she

held her breath. His reaction was immediate—his entire posture changed as he studied the drawing.

"This is …" When he paused, Nora felt awkward and shrugged. "Oh, I was just scribbling."

His eyes were fixed on the paper with an intensity that made her uncomfortable. "That's … the *Steadfast*." His voice was quiet, almost reverent. "My great-great-grandfather's ship."

Their eyes met. Neither spoke for a moment.

His eyebrows drew together as if he had a question, but he seemed afraid to say it.

His intensity unsettled her. "I just … that story got stuck in my mind, and … I could see it so clearly."

"I don't think you understand. Hold on." He went outside to his car and returned with a valise, his movements quick with barely contained excitement.

Nora waited while he thumbed through pages and finally pulled out a glossy print of a painting that matched her sketch with disturbing precision.

She leaned closer and studied it, her mouth going dry. "Well, I must have seen it somewhere and remembered."

He looked doubtful. "It's in the local lighthouse museum. Have you been there?"

The whole thing seemed too strange, too impossible. "No, I just moved here. I haven't had a chance to see much of the town." Nora's logical mind scrambled for explanations. "But it's just a ship in a storm. Your writing's so vivid I could visualize the scene." She gestured toward the window and its view of the harbor. "I mean, look out there. It's not hard to imagine a ship fighting those same waters."

Maddox shook his head slightly, still staring between her sketch and the museum print. "The chances of getting these details right by coincidence …" He trailed off, then looked up at her with those gray eyes that seemed to be trying to read her thoughts. "Well, that's some coincidence." He peered at her, and something in his intensity made her pulse quicken. His shoulders relaxed as if he'd made a decision to let the matter drop. "Anyway, there are some places you should see—coastal scenes that will take your breath away. When the light hits the water just right, it's magnificent. Perfect for an artist."

He seemed to be working up to something, so she did her best to sidestep it. "I'm sure I'll get around to seeing it all eventually, but for now, I have so much unpacking to do."

A glint in his eyes made it clear that he'd gotten the message. He was too smart not to recognize a polite deflection. "I imagine you do. Well, I'd like to talk about the house's history more sometime, but I'll give you some time to get properly settled. Here's my card. Give me a call when you're free for a chat."

A chat? She almost smiled at his careful choice of words as she took the card. "Sure."

"And if you change your mind about that tour, I've lived here all my life. I'd be happy to show you around." A smile tugged at the corner of his mouth. "No strings attached. Just consider it a welcome-to-Maine courtesy call."

He'd made the offer sound innocent enough—just a local guy showing a newcomer around. And Milt had assured her more than once that, in his words, Maddox was "one of the good ones." But something in the way he looked into her eyes, and the way her heart went weightless in response, convinced her that Maddox Hale could have too much effect on her. She didn't want that sort of complication right now.

She'd just uprooted her entire life, leaving everything familiar behind. The last thing she needed was to confuse her fresh start by getting entangled with someone she barely knew, no matter how good he looked in a sweater and jeans.

"That's very kind of you, but I'm still getting settled in. Maybe some other time?"

Something flickered across his face—understanding, maybe tinged with disappointment. "Sure. You've got a lot on your plate right now. If you do find anything related to the house's history, please give me a call. Even the smallest detail might be significant."

"I will. Thanks again for letting me read your manuscript."

"No problem," he said as he put the picture and his manuscript back into his valise. "I hope you find the inspiration you came for." With a nod that seemed to carry more weight than a simple goodbye, he turned and walked out the door.

Nora stood at the window and watched his car disappear down the road. Then she picked up her sketch of the *Steadfast* and studied the storm-tossed ship she had drawn. *Where did you come from?*

She set his business card on the coffee table and spent the rest of the morning unpacking, but her mind kept returning to the sketch and Maddox's reaction to it. She'd avoided her studio since the previous night—something about the room had felt too intense, too emotionally charged—but with the afternoon sunlight pouring in through the windows, she ventured back in to set up her easel and arrange her supplies.

The room seemed different in daylight. Peaceful. The harbor view from this angle was spectacular, and she could already envision the paintings she would create here. This was why she'd come to Maine—for moments like this, when the light and the setting aligned with her artistic vision.

By afternoon, though, she was restless. The house felt too quiet, too empty, despite her belongings now filling the rooms. She decided to explore the rest of the house more thoroughly.

She hadn't been to the basement yet. If it was musty and damp like most older houses, she doubted she'd use it for much, but it might be good for storage. The basement surprised her, though. The stone walls had been sealed and painted bright white, making the space feel clean and dry. Milt had mentioned waterproofing in one of their phone conversations, which she now appreciated more than ever.

The new furnace, water heater, and electrical panel took up one corner, their modern efficiency a stark contrast to the house's Victorian character. In the opposite corner, neatly arranged—probably by Milt's careful hand—she found some old pieces of furniture that looked broken and weathered beyond repair. They couldn't qualify as antiques, at least not valuable ones, but something about them suggested they'd been part of the house for a very long time.

The air down here carried a different scent than the rest of the house—not vanilla and cinnamon, but something fainter—fresh paint and the faint mustiness of the wood joists above that had absorbed decades of coastal dampness.

She approached the old furniture cautiously, not sure why she felt like she was intruding. A dented brass bed frame leaned against one wall, its headboard ornately carved but scarred with age. A wardrobe with a cracked mirror stood nearby, its doors slightly ajar to reveal empty darkness within.

But it was the small dresser that drew her attention. Its

drawers hung crooked, and the wood was water-stained and splitting in places. She pulled on the top drawer, which stuck and put up a fight, but Nora persisted. When it finally gave way, she was rewarded with the sight of a small wooden chest nestled in the back corner.

The moment her fingers touched the chest, she got that peculiar feeling again—the sensation of being watched, of not being alone in the quiet basement. The feeling was so strong that she actually turned around to check if someone had followed her downstairs, but she found only shadows and the soft hum of the furnace.

She quickly took the chest upstairs, eager to escape the sudden chill that seemed to have settled over the basement.

Back in the bright warmth of her living room, the chest seemed less ominous. From the smell of it, the box appeared to be cedar, with an intricately carved lid that opened more easily than she'd expected. The hinges, though tarnished with age, moved smoothly, as if someone had cared for this piece long after its contents had been forgotten.

Inside was a collection of items wrapped in once-white linen, now yellowed with time. Each bundle was tied with ribbon that had faded to the color of old roses, and something about the careful way everything had been preserved suggested these weren't just random possessions but treasured keepsakes.

Her heart hammered as she unwrapped the first bundle. Inside was a compass, its brass case polished smooth by countless hands. Despite its age, the needle still moved when she turned it, pointing north with the unwavering accuracy of a well-made instrument. Engraved on the back in elegant script were the initials "E.W." *Elias Wheeler?*

Beneath the compass was a ship's logbook, its leather cover cracked with age but still intact. The binding had been expertly done, built to withstand the harsh conditions of life at sea.

She opened it and squinted at the faded ink on the first page: *Property of Captain Elias Wheeler, Merchant Vessel Steadfast*.

"Oh my gosh," she whispered.

She turned the pages with trembling fingers, reading entries in Elias's careful script. They were routine and matter-of-fact in the way of working documents, but they painted a picture of a methodical, experienced captain who recorded everything with precise attention to detail.

The entries continued in the same vein—weather observations, navigation notes, and the daily routine of life aboard a working vessel. But reading them, Nora could see the character of the man who'd written them. Every entry was complete, every detail carefully noted. This wasn't the handwriting of someone careless or reckless.

Nora's hands shook as she set the logbook aside and unwrapped the next bundle. This one contained a letter—folded and never sent, dated September 30, 1871—three days before the shipwreck.

> *My Dearest Husband,*
>
> *I pray this letter finds you well and that the Steadfast's voyage has been profitable. The weather here has turned crisp, and I find myself eager for your return. I am so full of joy I can barely contain it. The garden is nearly finished for the season, though the late roses still bloom beautifully.*
>
> *On a more troubling note, Mr. Hawkins has been calling with supposed business inquiries, but I've grown uncomfortable with his manner. He lingers far too long and insists I call him Virgil, which I will not! And he asks impertinent questions about when you might return. I do not care for the way he looks at me. I know you would want me to speak up*

*about such things, so I had a word with Mr. Shaw. He
assured me he would address the matter. I feel much better
knowing I have taken proper steps.*

*I long for your safe return, my love. The house feels
empty without your laughter.*

All my love, your devoted wife

It stopped there, unfinished, unsigned. Below Mabel's
partial signature, in different ink, she had added a note.

*Too much worry for him. I'll tell him everything when
he's home.*

Nora was about to re-wrap everything when something
else caught her attention—something that had fallen from
the folds of the linen cloth. It was a small object that caught
the afternoon light from the window—a locket, its gold
surface tarnished but still beautiful, hanging from a delicate
chain that had somehow survived the decades without
breaking.

She lifted it up to the light, turning it until she found the
small clasp. Her hands were shaking as she opened it,
already suspecting somehow that whatever she found
inside would change everything.

The locket revealed a portrait painted on ivory—a
miniature so detailed and skillfully done that every feature
was crystal clear. It showed a young man with dark hair
and penetrating eyes, his face strong-jawed and serious, yet
softened by the hint of a smile at the corners of his mouth.

Nora couldn't breathe for a moment. She stared at the
tiny portrait, then looked toward the front door where
Maddox had stood just hours before, then back at the
locket.

The resemblance was impossible to dismiss.

The man in the portrait looked like Maddox—not just similar, not just a family resemblance, but identical. He had the same dark hair, the same eyes, the same facial structure, and even the same expression of quiet intensity that she'd seen when he looked at her sketch. As if responding to her recognition, the compass on the coffee table began to spin, its needle whirling in slow circles before gradually settling back to point north.

Nora's hands trembled as she re-wrapped the items with the same careful attention someone had used to preserve them generations ago. She had the strange feeling that she'd been intruding on something sacred, looking through someone else's most precious possessions and living in someone else's love story.

But this was her home now. She'd bought it, moved her life here, and filled it with her own belongings. Of course, other people had lived here before—she'd bought a house built in 1869. What did she expect? Still, the feeling persisted that she was somehow trespassing, that these artifacts belonged to a story that was still being written.

She sat for a moment, trying to calm her racing thoughts. "Stop imagining things," she said aloud to the empty room. "You'll be fine. You're an adult with a reasonable mind." She drew in a deep breath and let it out slowly.

But reasonable minds could differ.

She impulsively picked up her phone and found Maddox's business card on the coffee table. Her fingers hesitated over the numbers for just a moment, then she dialed.

"Hello, Maddox? It's Nora Delaney. I've found something I think you should see."

CHAPTER FIVE

NORA HAD BEEN STARING at the wooden chest's contents for three hours, and they were staring back.

The compass, logbook, letters, and locket lay spread across her coffee table like evidence at a crime scene, which, she supposed, they were—evidence of a love story cut short, a life ended too soon, and a mystery that had haunted her house for 150 years. She'd arranged and rearranged them, trying to make sense of the connection she felt to these artifacts, but all she'd accomplished was making herself feel more trapped in someone else's tragedy.

The locket portrait of Elias watched her from its small frame, his eyes achingly familiar. Every time she looked at it, she thought of Maddox. The resemblance was so uncanny that it left her unsettled.

She picked up the compass for the dozenth time and turned it over in her hands. The needle swung north, reliable after all these years, just as Elias had been reliable until that final, fatal night. Had he consulted this very compass as the *Steadfast* fought through the storm? Had his hands, so similar to Maddox's, gripped this same brass case as he tried to navigate home to Mabel?

A knock at the door made her jump. Through the window, she saw Maddox's tall frame on the porch, and relief flooded through her. She'd been buried in artifacts and the tragedy they represented, and she desperately needed an anchor to the present.

"Come in," she called, opening the door before he could knock again. "I'm so glad you're here."

His eyes, so like the ones in the locket, took in her appearance with concern. She probably looked as frazzled as she felt, still in yesterday's clothes, her hair pulled back in a messy ponytail.

As he stepped inside, his gaze moved to the coffee table with its careful display of artifacts. "This is quite a collection."

"I know." She gestured helplessly at the arrangement. "I keep thinking if I look at them long enough, they'll tell me their secrets. But all they're doing is making me feel sad for their loss."

Maddox moved to the coffee table, his approach reverent but controlled. When he picked up the logbook, his hands shook slightly. "This is Elias's handwriting. His actual words." He opened it and scanned the entries. "Look at these notations—every detail recorded, every weather observation precise. This is the work of a careful, methodical captain."

"Not someone who would sail recklessly into a storm," Nora agreed, settling beside him on the couch. She watched his face as he read and saw the emotion he was trying to contain. "You really believe he was set up, don't you?"

"I know he was. I just need to prove it." Maddox set the logbook down and picked up the locket, opening it to reveal the portrait. "Wow."

"I know," Nora said softly. "It's like looking at a photo of you, only it's from 150 years ago."

As they sat silently staring at the portrait, Nora was acutely aware of everything about Maddox—the way he'd rolled his shirtsleeves up to his elbows to reveal his strong forearms, the way his hair caught the light when he turned his head just so, and the hints of cedar and salt air mixed with his unique scent. It made her pulse quicken.

When he reached across the small table for his coffee, his fingers brushed hers, and the contact sent warmth shooting up her arm. His eyes met hers for just a moment longer than necessary, and she saw something flicker there —an awareness or interest—and she wondered if he felt the same electric connection she did. He slowly closed the locket and set it back on the table.

Nora tried to refocus her thoughts. "I can't shake the feeling that I'm supposed to do something with these," she said. "Finding them didn't feel like an accident. But I know that doesn't make any sense. Maybe I've been staring at these things too long." She stood to take her coffee mug to the kitchen, but a wave of dizziness overwhelmed her.

Maddox grasped her arm to steady her and then helped her sit down. When her vision cleared, she looked into his eyes, which were gentle and full of concern. "When's the last time you ate?"

She shook her head slowly.

"Or left this house?"

Nora thought back to the blur of moving trucks and unpacking boxes. "I went to the grocery store … maybe three days ago?"

"That doesn't count." He stood and extended his hand to her. "Come on. You need to breathe some sea air and see Mariner's Bluff properly. Not the tragic historical version, but the living, breathing town."

She looked at his outstretched hand, then back at the artifacts on her coffee table. The thought of leaving them felt wrong somehow, as if she were abandoning Elias and Mabel and the search for their truth.

"They'll still be here when we get back," Maddox said, reading her hesitation. "But you won't be any good to them if you make yourself sick obsessing over them."

The kindness in his voice helped her decide. She took his hand and let him pull her to her feet.

"Besides," he added with a smile that transformed his entire face, "you can't paint this place until you really know it. And I promise—no talk of shipwrecks or dead relatives until we get to the lighthouse museum. Deal?"

"Deal," she said, grabbing her jacket from the hook by the door. As they stepped outside, she filled her lungs with a deep breath of salt air and felt some of the tension leave her shoulders.

"Better?" Maddox asked.

"Much." She turned to lock the door, then hesitated. "Is it strange that I feel guilty leaving them?"

"Not strange at all. But Elias and Mabel waited 150 years. They can wait a few more hours."

The shore path that led from Nora's house down to the harbor was everything she'd imagined when she bought the property sight unseen. Rocky outcroppings jutted into the restless Atlantic, and tide pools nestled in the crevices between boulders, creating miniature worlds of sea anemones and hermit crabs. The afternoon breeze carried the scent of salt and seaweed, and gulls wheeled overhead, their cries mixing with the rhythm of waves against stone.

"This is where I come when the research gets too heavy," Maddox said, scrambling down to a tide pool and pointing out a bright orange starfish clinging to the rocks.

"I wanted to be a marine biologist before I got seduced by dusty archives."

"What changed your mind?" Nora asked, carefully picking her way across the wet rocks. The ocean air was already clearing her head, making the morning's preoccupation with the artifacts feel distant and manageable.

"Family history called louder than science, I guess." He skipped a flat stone across the water, and she counted four skips before it sank. "Though sometimes I wonder if Miranda was right—if I chose the past because it felt safer than building a future."

The vulnerability in his admission warmed her. She bent and selected her own stone, trying to copy his technique. Her stone managed two skips before disappearing beneath the waves.

"Better than my usual zero," she said, and he laughed.

"It's all in the wrist. Here, like this." He moved behind her, his hand covering hers as he adjusted her grip. The contact sent warmth through her that she hadn't expected. "Now, sidearm, parallel to the water."

Her next attempt achieved three skips, and she turned to grin at him in triumph, suddenly aware of how close he was standing. For a moment, they were just a man and a woman on a beautiful shore, not two strangers bound together by mystery and tragedy.

"I should probably admit something," Nora said as they continued walking. "This is going to sound weird, but I've been feeling haunted by the house. Not just the artifacts—the whole place. Like it's trying to tell me something, but I don't speak the language."

Instead of looking at her like she was crazy, Maddox nodded thoughtfully. "Old houses have their own personalities. And that one has seen more than its share of joy and sorrow."

"You don't think I'm losing my mind?"

"Not even close. I think you're sensitive to things other people miss. It's probably what makes you such a good artist."

They encountered one of the locals, Mrs. Foster, near the harbor, walking her ancient golden retriever at a pace that accommodated the dog's arthritic joints. Maddox introduced Nora, and within minutes, Mrs. Foster was treating her like she'd lived in town for years.

"You simply must come to book club next Thursday," the older woman insisted. "Perfect timing—we're about to choose our next book, and we need fresh perspectives. Too many of us are stuck in our ways."

"I'd love to," Nora said, surprising herself.

As they continued toward the harbor, she realized she and Maddox had fallen into step with each other, walking closer than they had when they started. The awkward politeness from yesterday had given way to something more comfortable.

"How's your arthritis treating you, Mrs. Foster?" Maddox called back to the older woman.

"Oh, you know how it is, dear. Some days are better than others. But this weather's been kind."

"That's good to hear. Give my best to Harold."

It was a small interaction, but it revealed something important about Maddox's character. He wasn't just being polite—he genuinely cared about people, remembered details about their lives, and checked on them with interest.

"You're not what I expected," Nora said once Mrs. Foster was out of earshot.

"What did you expect?"

"I don't know. Someone more … preoccupied, I guess. Too caught up in your studies to be … social."

"Oh," he said, frowning. "Well, I can get pretty focused,

but not in the way people think. I'm acutely aware of the present, but injustice disturbs me, whether it's in the past or the present. I don't think the truth should stay buried."

"And now?"

"Now I'm wondering if I've been going about it all wrong. Fighting this battle alone, using it to avoid building anything real in the present." He glanced at her sideways. "Meeting you has made me think differently about some things."

Nora was about to ask how, when Maddox grinned toward the harbor.

The working harbor was a revelation. Unlike the romantic postcard version Nora had imagined, this was a place of serious business—fishing boats heading out for afternoon runs, lobster traps stacked on the docks, and men in yellow rain gear discussing weather, catches, and the price of fuel.

"Maddox!" A weathered man in his sixties waved from the deck of a boat called *Sarah's Pride*. "Come help me with this, would you?"

Without hesitation, Maddox jogged over to help Captain Joe Leighton lift a heavy crate from the boat to the dock. Nora watched the easy way he moved, the natural strength in his shoulders, and the way the other fishermen accepted his help without question.

"Who's your friend?" Joe asked, nodding toward Nora with a smile.

"Joe Leighton, meet Nora Delaney. She just bought the Captain's Watch up on Mariner's Bluff."

"No kidding?" Joe's face lit up with interest. "Beautiful place. My great-grandfather used to tell stories about the folks who lived there back in the day. He said the captain who owned it was a good man—steady as she goes, that one."

"Elias Wheeler," Maddox said, and Nora heard the hope in his voice.

"That's the one. Went down in that storm back in 1871. But according to my great-granddad, he was no fool. He knew these waters better than most." Joe gave Maddox a meaningful look. "It's not the first time you and I have talked about this, is it?"

"No, sir."

"Well, I still say the same thing I said before. That official story never sat right with the old-timers. Of course, the inquiry blamed it on him being desperate to get home to his wife—said she was expecting and he took foolish risks in his eagerness to reach her. But they knew Captain Wheeler and knew his reputation. Something else had to have happened that night."

Nora felt a thrill of vindication. This wasn't just Maddox's fixation. Other people had always questioned the official narrative.

"What kind of stories did your great-grandfather tell?" she asked.

"Oh, the usual harbor gossip. But he always said the light went out that night. He swore he saw it himself from his house up on Pine Street. One minute it was there; the next minute it wasn't." Joe shrugged. "Of course, nobody believed him then. The official report said the light was working fine."

"Did he say anything else about that night?" Maddox pressed.

"Just that he never trusted the lighthouse keeper after that. He said Jasper Shaw got real peculiar after the wreck. He got jumpy and nervous and started drinking heavily. But that's old gossip, and Shaw's been dead near a century now."

As they walked away from the docks, Nora slipped her

hand through Maddox's arm without thinking about it. The gesture felt natural, comfortable, like something she'd been doing for years.

"You see?" she said. "People have always known you were right."

"Some people. But not the ones who matter to historians." His voice carried old hurt and old frustration. "Academic careers aren't built on harbor gossip and family stories."

"Maybe that's the problem with academic careers."

He stopped walking and peered into her eyes. "You really believe this, don't you? It's not just politeness or curiosity."

"I believe you," she said simply. "I believe Elias was innocent, and I believe someone covered up the truth. And I think we're going to prove it."

The smile that spread across his face was like sunrise— slow, warm, and transforming. "We?"

"We," she confirmed. "That is, if you'd like a partner who doesn't know the first thing about maritime history but has good instincts and a stubborn streak."

"I'd like that very much," he said quietly.

"Come here," Maddox said as they walked up the road. "I want to show you something."

He led her to where Mariner's Bluff Cemetery sat on a gentle slope overlooking the harbor. The 150-year-old headstones cast long shadows in the afternoon light, many bearing maritime motifs—anchors, ships, lighthouse beams —testaments to lives shaped by the sea.

"There," Maddox said, pointing toward a section of graves near a gnarled maple tree. "The Wheeler plot."

They walked toward the weathered stones. Elias's monument was larger, a simple granite marker that read:

CAPTAIN ELIAS WHEELER Beloved Husband 1840–1871 Lost at Sea

Beside Elias's grave stood a smaller stone, its inscription faded but still legible:

MABEL WHEELER Beloved Wife 1849–1871 "She died of a broken heart."

And there, nestled close to Mabel's grave, was a tiny headstone no larger than a book:

BABY WHEELER October 1871 "Too soon for this world."

Nora felt her breath catch. "She lost the baby."

"The stress and the grief must have been unbearable," Maddox said gently. "She couldn't survive losing them both."

They stood in silence for a moment, the weight of the tragedy settling over them. Here lay the real cost of whatever had happened that night—not just the seven men who died in the shipwreck, but a young woman and her unborn child.

As if in response to their presence, a warm breeze stirred around them. The afternoon light seemed to glow more warmly, and for a moment, the cemetery felt not sad but peaceful.

LUNCH AT SALTY'S Lobster Shack felt like a celebration, though Nora couldn't quite say what they were celebrating. The restaurant was everything she'd hoped for—weathered wood tables overlooking the water, the smell of fresh seafood and salt air, and the kind of casual atmosphere that made everyone feel welcome.

"First rule of Maine lobster rolls," Maddox said with mock seriousness as their food arrived. "No mixing with Connecticut-style hot lobster rolls. That's grounds for deportation."

"Noted," Nora said, taking her first bite of the cold lobster salad piled into a buttered bun. "Oh my gosh, this is incredible."

"Wait until you try the blueberry pie. Judy makes it from scratch every morning."

Their waitress, a woman in her fifties with kind eyes and efficient movements, greeted Maddox like family and treated Nora like she'd been coming here for years. It was another small sign of how embedded Maddox was in this community and how much people liked him.

"So what's your story?" Nora asked as she ate a french fry. "I mean, I know about the research and the shipwreck, but what about the rest? Family? Hobbies? Secret talents?"

"Boring academic stuff, mostly. I grew up here, went away to college, and came back to teach at Rockland. Thought I'd have a quiet career writing books about maritime history that twelve people would read." He paused, considering. "The secret talent is my cooking. I'm remarkably bad at it."

"What about your family? Do they live here too?"

"My parents retired to Florida last year. They got tired of waiting for me to give them grandchildren and decided to pursue their own adventures." There was humor in his voice, but Nora caught an undercurrent of hurt. "They think my research is a waste of time. My mother's exact words were 'chasing ghosts instead of living with the living.'"

"And Miranda?"

"Ex-girlfriend. She left because she said I cared more about proving myself right than building a life with her." He met Nora's eyes across the table. "She might have had a point."

"Past tense," Nora said gently. "Things change. People change."

"What about you? What made you pack up your life and move to the middle of nowhere, Maine?"

Nora considered her answer, surprised by how much she wanted to be honest with him. The true answer was loneliness, but she wasn't ready to admit that to him. "I needed a change. Desperately. I spent three years in New York painting other people's visions, living in other people's stories. The commercial work was soul-crushing, but the alternative was painting for myself and having no money for rent."

"What kind of painting did you want to do?"

"Maritime scenes, actually. Storms, shipwrecks, and lighthouses. I've always been drawn to them, but I never understood quite how much until I found those artifacts."

She turned to take in the view. The harbor spread out before her like a living masterpiece, all blues and grays and white sailboat masts bobbing at their moorings. Fishing boats dotted the water, some heading out for evening runs, others already returning with their catch. In the distance, a red-roofed lighthouse stood perched on a rocky outcropping where the harbor met the endless expanse of the Atlantic.

The sight called to something deep inside her—the part of her soul that had always been drawn to the ocean, to the endless horizon where the sky met the water. Her maritime paintings, the ones she created for herself rather than for clients, always featured scenes like this—lonely lighthouses standing guard against storms and ships cutting through heavy seas toward home—the eternal dance between human hope and nature's power.

She gestured toward the harbor, where fishing boats bobbed at their moorings. "That's what I moved here to find—inspiration for the art I've been longing to paint. But I've been so busy painting the art people want that I lost sight of the art in my soul." Images of cheerful roosters on kitchen towels and cottage gardens on coffee mugs flashed through her mind.

Maddox leaned his chin on his hand and gazed thoughtfully. "Why here? Why the sea?"

Nora tried to put into words the pull she'd always felt toward maritime scenes. "I think I've longed for the sea all my life." It was rooted in a childhood memory she treasured above all others, and the thought made her smile.

"My grandmother's small house was filled with the things we accumulate over the span of a long life, but one thing captured my eight-year-old's imagination. A simple seascape hung over the faded velvet sofa. Nothing fancy—just a small sailboat on calm blue water with sunlight dancing on the waves, but it spoke to me in a language I didn't yet understand.

"Once I asked her about it, and she told me, 'That's where I met your grandfather. Right there on that exact beach. He was so handsome in his Navy uniform, and I knew the moment I saw him he was going to sail right into my heart and change everything.'" She looked at Maddox and smiled. "Romantic, isn't it?"

"Anyway, after she died, the painting disappeared—probably into some relative's garage sale. But that feeling it gave me never faded. All that hope and adventure waiting somewhere beyond the horizon." She sighed. "So here I am. Trying to recapture that feeling of standing on the edge of

forever, of believing that the next tide might bring everything you'd been waiting for."

Nora tossed her head back and laughed. "Listen to me—
waxing all artsy."

Maddox didn't laugh with her. "No, I'm fascinated."

Nora's eyebrows drew together. "Now you're just being
nice."

A glint came to his eyes. "I've been known to be nice on
occasion."

"Have you?" Her smile faded as she gazed into his eyes.
She could lose herself there if she wasn't careful. She
averted her gaze as a thought came to mind that she chose
not to share. The truth was, she'd bought the house partly
because she was lonely and partly because she was hoping
to find some kind of romantic story to live in instead of the
ones she dreamed up on canvas.

A smile started to form as he said, "Depending on who
you ask, those occasions might be rare." The next instant,
the smile was gone, and he peered into her eyes. "I'm glad
that you're here."

Their eyes met across the table, and Nora felt that same
electric awareness she'd experienced on the shore when
he'd helped her skip stones. But this was deeper, more
meaningful—the recognition that they understood one
another. They might even be good for each other, each
bringing out something in the other that was missing
before.

"Another round?" Judy asked, appearing with the
coffee pot.

"Please," Maddox said, not breaking eye contact with
Nora.

As Judy refilled their cups, she grinned at them with
obvious approval. "Nice to see you with such good
company, Maddox. About time you brought a girl around."

After she left, Nora laughed. "Does everyone in town know your business?"

"Pretty much. It's the price of living in a place where your high school English teacher still corrects your grammar at the grocery store."

"Do you ever think about leaving?"

"I used to. When the academic career fell apart, when Miranda left, when it seemed like everyone thought I was crazy. But this is home. These people, this place—they're part of me." He leaned back in his chair, studying her face. "What about you? Think you'll stay?"

"Ask me again in six months," Nora said. "But right now, sitting here with you, watching those boats come in … I can't imagine being anywhere else."

The town's main street was a perfect blend of tourist charm and local business. Maddox showed her his favorite spots—the bookstore where he admitted he sometimes hid from his problems, the art supply store where the owner immediately adopted Nora as a new favorite customer, and the general store where he knew everyone who worked there by name and always bought Girl Scout cookies from every kid in town.

"Let me guess," Nora said as they walked between shops, their shoulders brushing. "You're the guy who helps elderly neighbors carry their groceries and never misses a town meeting."

"Guilty as charged. Though in my defense, Mrs. Potter's groceries are really heavy, and town meetings are where all the best gossip happens."

She watched him joke with the teenage cashier at the general store about her upcoming prom and saw the way his face lit up when he talked to people and the interest he showed in their lives. This wasn't the obsessed, isolated academic she'd expected. This was a man who was deeply connected to his community, who cared about people and was cared for in return.

"You surprise me," she said again as they left the store.

"How so?"

"I don't know. I guess I thought you'd be more of a loner."

He winced. "So you had me profiled as a serial killer type?"

"No!" she insisted, then saw his eye crinkle as a laugh quickly followed.

Nora forced a serious expression. "Milt assured me you weren't."

Now it was Maddox's turn for surprise. "You asked him?"

After a moment, Nora let out a laugh. "Not in so many words."

He shook his head. "Note to self: Make better first impressions."

Nora gazed at him, enjoying a glimpse of uncertainty in this man who otherwise functioned with such singular purpose.

His smile faded. "Maybe I've been too fixed on the past. The present has a lot to offer." As he gazed at her, the words hung between them, honest and vulnerable. The oppressive feeling she'd had in the house that morning had lifted as though hope were taking root.

She said softly, "I know what you mean. I'm beginning to realize there's a world outside of my paintings."

When she feared she was revealing too much too soon, Nora averted her eyes to the bookstore window beside them. Their reflections looked back at them—a tall man and a woman with dark hair, standing close enough to touch, looking at each other like they were seeing something new and wonderful. For a moment, the reflection looked like a photograph of two people who belonged together.

"Should we head to the lighthouse museum?" Maddox asked, his voice slightly rough.

"Yes," Nora said. "I think it's time."

The lighthouse museum was smaller than Nora had expected, housed in the base of the lighthouse she could see from her bedroom window. The elderly volunteer, a woman named Hilda, greeted Maddox like an old friend and welcomed Nora with the warmth she was beginning to recognize as typically Maine.

"We've got some new additions to the 1871 storm display," Hilda said, leading them to a glass case near the back of the room. "The family donated a whole box of items last week. They found them cleaning out their great-great-grandmother's attic."

Nora's pulse quickened as she looked at the display. There was the painting that matched her sketch—the *Steadfast* fighting through towering waves, the lighthouse conspicuously dark in the background. But there were new items too: a pressed flower in a small frame, its petals still faintly purple after 150 years, and a family Bible open to a page with handwritten entries.

"That flower came from someone's garden," Hilda explained. "The same type that grew wild around here in the 1870s. And the Bible belonged to the lighthouse keeper's family—the Shaws. Look at the dates of the family entries."

Nora leaned closer, studying the careful script. Birth dates, death dates, marriage records. And in the margin was an entry in different handwriting:

God forgive me for what I have done.

Maddox's intake of breath was sharp. "That's ... interesting timing."

Hilda said, "But we haven't had time to go through all the family records yet. So much came in at once."

"Oh, and there's one more piece," Hilda added, reaching into the display case. "This was wrapped separately in the donation box." She carefully lifted out a small object—a miniature portrait on a copper disc, no more than three inches across, set in a simple gold frame. The surface had the distinctive glossy, jewel-like appearance of fired enamel and showed a young woman with dark hair and luminous eyes, painted with exquisite detail that seemed to glow from within the glass-smooth surface.

"This is exquisite," Nora breathed, leaning closer to study the fine work. The woman in the portrait was beautiful, but more than that—she was alive with hope and love, her expression soft and radiant. The enamel technique gave her skin an almost luminous quality, as if lit from within.

"The family thought it might have belonged to Captain Wheeler," Hilda said. "It was found on the shore near the wreckage. These enamel miniatures were quite popular with sea captains—the copper base and fired glass surface could survive almost anything, unlike watercolor portraits. Perfect for long voyages. The back has the initials 'M.W.'"

"Mabel," Maddox said, his voice filled with wonder. "That's Mabel."

Nora stared at the miniature, feeling that familiar artistic stirring. This wasn't the tragic victim she'd imagined from reading Maddox's manuscript. This was a young woman deeply in love, someone who had posed for this portrait knowing it would be treasured by her husband during his long voyages.

"Could I ..." Nora hesitated, then pulled out her phone.

"Would it be okay if I took a few photos? For reference? As an artist, I mean."

"Of course, dear," Hilda said. "Just no flash—these old paints are sensitive to light."

Nora photographed the miniature from several angles, capturing the way the enamel surface caught and reflected the museum's lighting. The fired glass gave Mabel's features an almost ethereal quality that Nora could already envision translating into a larger painting. As she studied the image on her phone screen, she longed to bring this vibrant, hopeful young woman to life on canvas—Mabel as she had been, not as history had left her.

Hilda listened to their conversation with growing interest. "You know, there are more family papers in the donation. Letters, journals, household records. Most of it's been boxed up in our storage room—we just don't have space to display everything."

"Could we look through them?" Maddox asked.

"Of course, dear. Though you'll have to come back another day. I'm closing up in a few minutes."

As they walked back toward Nora's house, the late afternoon light painting everything in soft hues, both of them were quiet. They'd found something—not definitive proof yet, but a thread that could lead to it.

"You really think we can do this?" Nora said as her house came into view. "Solve a 150-year-old mystery?"

"I really think we can try," Maddox said.

They stopped at her porch steps, neither of them eager to end the day. Nora realized the oppressive feeling from that morning was gone. The house felt peaceful now.

"Thank you," she said, turning to face him. "For getting me out of my own head today. I loved seeing your world. It's helped me feel like I belong."

"I'm the one who should thank you for …" He paused,

searching for words. "For making me feel like this quest isn't futile. Or maybe it's just that misery loves company." A smile began to form but was gone the next second. "You're good company."

They stood facing each other at the gate, the space between them charged with longing. For a moment, Nora thought he might kiss her. She wanted him to.

Instead, he averted his gaze. "So, tomorrow let's go through those family papers and track down any leads."

With that, the moment passed, and disappointment mixed with relief. "Okay." Nora settled for a feeling of keen satisfaction at the thought of working together. For now, that was enough. It was too soon to admit it. She barely knew Maddox, but the more she discovered, the more she wanted to know.

As his car disappeared down the road, Nora went inside. The house felt normal again. Maddox had been right. All she'd needed was some fresh air and a day out.

Tomorrow, they would resume working together. But tonight, for the first time since arriving in Maine, Nora felt truly at home.

CHAPTER SIX

NORA WAS ARRANGING Elias's artifacts on her coffee table, preparing for another day of investigation with Maddox, when her phone rang.

"Hey, what's up?" She answered, cradling the phone between her shoulder and ear while positioning the compass next to the logbook.

"Surprise! I'm in your driveway. Don't look out the window—I want to see your face when I knock."

"What?" Nora nearly dropped the phone. "Caroline, what are you doing here?"

"Escaping the concrete jungle. You know how unbearable the city gets in August. I rented a car, drove up the coast, spent the night in Boothbay Harbor—which is adorable, by the way—and decided to surprise my best friend in her new house." The sound of a car door slamming punctuated her words. "Now stop asking questions and come let me in!"

The line went dead, and Nora stared at her phone in shock. Caroline was here. Right now. She glanced at the artifacts spread across her coffee table, at the research notes she'd been making, and at the general state of a house that still looked like someone was in the middle of moving in.

The knock came as promised—Caroline's signature rapid-fire rhythm that managed to sound both imperious and cheerful at the same time.

Nora opened the door to find her best friend standing on the porch with an overnight bag slung over her shoulder and a huge grin on her face. Caroline wore her straight blonde hair twisted up into one of those messy buns that somehow managed to look perfectly intentional, designer glasses perched on her nose, and the kind of effortlessly chic outfit that only worked if you had Caroline's confidence and credit card.

"Oh my gosh, Nora!" Caroline dropped her bag and pulled her into a fierce hug. "You look amazing. Maine air agrees with you."

"I can't believe you're here," Nora said, squeezing her back. Despite the surprise, she felt a rush of pure joy at seeing her friend. "When did you decide to do this?"

"Yesterday morning. I was melting on the subway platform with the scent of urine wafting through the air, cursing August in Manhattan, and I thought, 'Caroline, you have vacation days. Your best friend just moved to a stunning house in a beautiful state. What are you waiting for?'" She stepped back to study Nora's face. "You do look good, though. Relaxed. When's the last time I saw you without that little worry line between your eyebrows?"

Caroline picked up her bag and swept past Nora into the house, her gaze cataloging everything with the efficiency of someone who'd been Nora's friend for over a decade.

"Oh, wow! This place is gorgeous," she breathed, taking in the soaring ceilings and harbor view. "The photos didn't do it justice. But what's all this?" She'd spotted the artifacts on the coffee table—the compass, logbook, letters, and locket arranged like evidence at a crime scene.

"Oh, that's …" Nora hesitated. How did you explain to your practical, city-dwelling best friend that you'd found 150-year-old love letters in your basement and were now investigating a historical mystery with a man who looked exactly like a dead sea captain?

"I found some things that belonged to previous owners. Historical stuff."

"Mm-hmm." Caroline was studying the display with the sharp attention she usually reserved for analyzing marketing campaigns. "And you've been playing detective?"

"Something like that. Coffee? I just made a fresh pot."

"Gosh, yes. Real coffee, not that burnt swill I usually drink at the office."

As Nora busied herself in the kitchen, Caroline continued her exploration of the main floor, her voice carrying from room to room.

"I have to say, I'm impressed. This doesn't look like the impulse purchase of someone having a breakdown. It looks like …" She appeared in the kitchen doorway. "Like home. Like you actually found what you were looking for."

Nora felt a warmth spread through her chest. "I think maybe I did."

"And the work situation? You're painting again?"

"Every day." Nora handed Caroline a mug and led her back to the living room. "I've got a studio upstairs with the most incredible light. I'm working on a series about maritime history—storms, shipwrecks, and lighthouses. Things I've always wanted to paint but never had the time to try."

"That's wonderful." Caroline settled into the window seat, curling her legs under her. "I was worried you'd be up here second-guessing everything, buried in boxes, wondering what the hell you'd done."

"I did wonder that. The first day. But then ..." Nora trailed off, not sure how to explain the sense of rightness she'd found here, the way the house seemed to welcome her, or the way Maddox had appeared at exactly the right moment.

"Then what?"

Before Nora could answer, her phone rang. Maddox's name appeared on the screen, and she felt that familiar little flutter of anticipation.

"Sorry, I should take this," she said to Caroline, who was watching with suddenly sharp interest.

"Good morning," Nora answered, trying to sound casual.

"Morning." Maddox sounded warm with the unvoiced affection that seemed to be growing between them. "Ready for another day of mystery-solving? I've got the museum volunteer meeting us at ten with those Shaw family papers."

Nora felt heat rise in her cheeks and was acutely aware of Caroline's eagle-eyed attention. "Actually, I need to postpone. My friend Caroline surprised me with a visit—she drove up from New York."

"The best friend? The one who questioned your sanity for buying your house?"

"That's the one." Nora couldn't help smiling at his teasing tone.

"Well, tell her I said she has excellent taste in friends. And don't worry about today—Dorothy can reschedule. Family first."

"She's not really family—"

"Friends who drive eight hours to surprise you are de facto family," Maddox said firmly. "Besides, it'll give me time to do some research on those Bible entries we found. Maybe I can track down more Shaw family records."

"You don't have to—"

"I want to. This is our project now, remember? I'll call you tonight to check in and see how the visit's going."

"Okay." Nora's voice came out softer than she'd intended, and she saw Caroline's eyebrows rise.

"Enjoy your friend. And Nora?"

"Yeah?"

"Yesterday was perfect. I'm looking forward to more of the same."

The line went dead, leaving Nora staring at her phone with what she was sure must look like unabashed happiness.

Caroline set down her coffee mug with deliberate precision.

"Okay," she said, her voice carrying the tone Nora recognized from their college days when Caroline was about to stage an intervention. "Who the hell was that, and why are you glowing like a teenager who just got asked to prom?"

"That was Maddox," Nora said, trying for casual and failing. "He's helping me research the history of the house."

"Uh-huh." Caroline pushed her glasses up her nose, a gesture Nora knew meant her friend was shifting into analysis mode. "And what are you researching—the history of the horizontal Mambo? Sideways salsa? Perpendicular pas de deux?"

"It's not like that."

"Really? Because your face says it's exactly like that." Caroline leaned forward, studying Nora with the intensity she usually reserved for dissecting marketing campaigns. "How long have you known this guy?"

"A few weeks."

"A few weeks." Caroline repeated the words slowly, as if testing their weight. "And you're already glowing when he calls?" Caroline's voice held a note of concern that made Nora bristle. "Nora, honey, please tell me you're not doing what I think you're doing."

"What do you think I'm doing?"

"Living out some romantic fantasy. You know—lonely city girl moves to picturesque coastal town and immediately falls for the first handsome stud who sweeps her off her feet."

"Since when do you have a problem with handsome studs?"

"Since they threaten to hurt my best friend."

"Nobody's threatening to hurt anyone, Caroline. I think somebody's overreacting."

Caroline gestured toward the artifacts on the coffee table. "and this whole archaeological dig of yours seems kind of sketchy."

Nora looked at her friend with as much patience as she could muster. "I moved into an old house, and it has a history. What's wrong with that?"

"I love the house. It's the man I have doubts about." Caroline's tone was gentle but relentless. "You've been single for three years, Nora. Three years of brushing off perfectly decent guys because something was always missing. But you move here, and before you unpack, Mr. Right shows up on your doorstep?"

"You don't even know him."

"I know you. I know that you bought this house partly because you wanted inspiration for your art, but partly because you were lonely." Caroline's voice softened. "And there's nothing wrong with that, but there are men who prey on that sort of thing."

"Maddox isn't like that."

"Of course he isn't. I'm sure he's wonderful. Charming, intelligent, and probably looks like he stepped out of a men's sports magazine." Caroline stood and moved to the window, looking out at the harbor view. "But Nora, you don't really know anything about him."

"I know enough."

Caroline turned back to face her, and Nora saw worry in her friend's eyes. "Do you? Or do you know the version of himself he's chosen to show you? Look, all I'm saying is, if he starts asking for money, do not walk—run away."

Before Nora could respond, something strange happened. The compass on the coffee table began to vibrate and spin, its needle rotating wildly instead of pointing north. Both women stared at it.

"That's ... odd," Caroline said slowly.

"It does that sometimes," Nora said, though she sounded uncertain even to herself. "I think there's a magnetic field here or something."

"Nora, magnetic fields don't make compasses go off like cartoon alarm clocks."

"Well... it's probably just this old house settling."

Caroline raised an eyebrow doubtfully and approached the coffee table cautiously. "How long has this been happening?"

"Since I found it in the basement."

A book fell off the shelf with a loud thud at Caroline's feet, making both women jump.

Caroline stared at the fallen book, then at Nora. "Okay, what the hell is going on in this house?"

"Nothing's going on. It's just—"

"Books don't just randomly leap off bookcases, and compasses don't spin for no reason." Caroline's voice was rising slightly. "And you've been living here alone with ... all this going on?"

"Nothing's going on. It's an old house, and we're getting used to each other."

"Getting used to each other?" Caroline's eyes widened. "Nora, this isn't normal."

"I know it must sound like—"

Caroline shook her head. "It sounds like you're so desperate to believe that you've found your dream home and your dream life where everything's perfect that you're ignoring some obvious red flags." She sank back into the window seat, her perfectly composed facade finally showing cracks. "A mysterious hot guy—"

Nora protested, "Who said he was hot?"

"Your blushing face did. So you've got a brooding, hot guy and an old—let's be honest—haunted house. Oh, and a romantic historical mystery. Do you hear yourself, Nora?"

Nora felt frustrated and hurt. "I hear you more or less calling me crazy."

"I'm calling you human. You were lonely and isolated in New York, and now you've found this place that seems to offer everything you were missing. But honey, real life doesn't work like fairy tales. There's always more to the story."

Nora glanced at the compass, which had stopped spinning and was now pointing steadily north again, as if nothing had happened. The house fell silent around them.

"I know you're trying to protect me," Nora said. "But I'm not some naive girl who's never been hurt before. I know the difference between fantasy and reality."

"Do you?" Caroline's question was gentle but pointed. "Because from where I'm sitting, it looks like you've convinced yourself that a man you barely know is your perfect partner, that a house that looks like last week's episode of *Ghost Hunters* is your dream home, and that some 150-year-old unsolved mystery is your calling in life. All in the span of three weeks."

Nora wanted to argue and wanted to defend her choices and her feelings. But Caroline's words hit closer to home than she wanted to admit. Was she projecting fantasies onto Maddox? Was she so desperate to belong somewhere that she'd ignored obvious warning signs?

"What if you're wrong?" Nora asked. "What if this really is where I'm supposed to be?"

"Then I'll be the first to admit it and apologize," Caroline said. "But promise me you'll be careful. Promise me you won't make any major decisions based on a week's worth of feelings."

Nora looked around her living room—at the artifacts that had started this whole adventure, at the view of the harbor that called to her artist's soul, at the space that had felt like home from the moment she'd walked through the door.

"I'm not making any major decisions." But Caroline's stern look was relentless. "Okay, I promise," she said, but the words felt heavy.

Caroline nodded, some of the tension leaving her shoulders. "Good. Now, tell me more about this Maddox. And I want details—not just the romantic highlights."

Nora curled up in the corner of the couch. Where did she even start? "He's a historian. He was researching his great-great-grandfather, who used to live in this house."

Caroline frowned. "So he just stopped by to welcome you to the old family home?"

"No. He came because his great-great-grandfather's pocket watch started working again when he stopped by the property earlier."

"His pocket watch started working." Caroline's tone

was neutral. "Because of the house. Okay ... And why had he stopped by in the first place?"

"Oh. Well, he's writing a book about a shipwreck from 1871. His ancestor was the captain who died, and Maddox believes the official story is wrong—that someone covered up what really happened." Ignoring Caroline's skepticism, Nora continued. "He's spent years researching it, trying to clear his family name."

"And you believe him?"

"I do. The artifacts I found prove his ancestor was a careful, methodical captain. His logbook entries and letters don't match the official story of a reckless man who sailed into a storm."

Caroline leaned forward. "Nora, why are you so intent upon solving this old mystery?"

"Because it's connected to my house. We found new evidence yesterday. At the lighthouse museum, there was a photograph of the lighthouse keeper's wife. There was something about the way she looked, like she was troubled or even guilty."

Caroline winced. "Or maybe she just remembered she'd left the oven on."

"There was also a note in her Bible. 'God forgive me for what I have done.'"

"Okay, I get it. New place. Time on your hands. Why not play Nancy Drew?" The words came out sharper than Caroline probably intended, and she immediately softened her tone. "I'm sorry. I just ... this is a lot, Nora."

"I know it must sound like it."

"Because it is. Put yourself in my place. You move to a small town and immediately partner up with a handsome stranger to solve historical mysteries? What would you think?"

"I would think it was nice that you're happy."

"I will too, as soon as I know that you're safe."

Just when Nora was beginning to feel annoyed with her friend, she saw the concern in her eyes and appreciated the fact that she meant well. "Caroline. Trust me. I'm safe."

Caroline's shoulders relaxed just a bit. "All right, tell me about him—not just his research skills, but about him as a person."

Nora hesitated, trying to separate her feelings from the facts. "He's kind. Yesterday, he showed me around town and introduced me to people. Everyone seemed to know him, and he asked about them and their families. He helped an older fisherman lift some crates. Caroline, he wasn't putting on a show. He's kind, and people like him."

"That's good. What else?"

"He's smart and funny. He can't cook, apparently." Nora smiled despite herself. "He used to want to be a marine biologist before he was drawn to historical research. He taught me how to skip stones."

"And his romantic history?"

The question made Nora uncomfortable, but she pressed on, determined to quell her friend's fears. "He had a girlfriend named Miranda, but they've broken up."

"And they broke up because …?"

Now Nora wished she could change the subject, but it was too late. "Because … she thought he was too obsessed with his research."

"Uh-huh." Caroline's expression sharpened. "So he has a pattern of placing relationships second."

"One instance isn't a pattern." Nora heard how defensive she sounded, but she couldn't help herself.

"Maybe. But so far your relationship with him—"

"I wouldn't call it a relationship. Yet."

Caroline nodded. "Fair enough. But so far everything you're telling me centers on his research."

"I'm obviously not explaining this well. His ex didn't believe in what he was doing."

"Why not?"

"I don't know." Nora reminded herself that Caroline was simply being a caring friend looking out for her. But this conversation was becoming increasingly unpleasant. "Apparently, she accused him of chasing ghosts instead of living in the present."

"And you're different how?"

The question hung in the air between them. Nora felt a flicker of doubt—was she just Miranda's replacement, another woman willing to enable Maddox's obsession?

"I believe in his work," she said finally. "I think what he's doing matters."

"Would you believe that as much if he weren't smokin' hot?"

Nora said, "I think so." She couldn't hold back the smile that was forming. "But it doesn't hurt that he's smokin' hot." They shared a laugh, and to Nora's relief, it eased the tension.

Caroline stood and went to the coffee table and studied the artifacts. "These are beautiful. They're probably valuable. I'm sure it's interesting finding things like this in your basement. But Nora, finding old letters in your basement doesn't make you a historian. And being attracted to a man doesn't make his quest your calling."

"What if it does, though? What if I'm supposed to be here—to help him?"

"Supposed to, according to whom? Some cosmic plan?"

Caroline didn't understand. That much was clear. The problem was, Nora didn't understand either, so she let the question go unanswered.

Caroline picked up the locket, opening it to reveal Elias's portrait. "Oh my gosh."

Nora smiled. "Not bad, huh?"

Caroline grinned. "Not bad at all."

"He looks just like Maddox."

"Wow. Well, I approve—looks-wise, anyway." Caroline stared at the miniature painting, then looked up at Nora with concern. "Honey, this is getting into really strange territory. The resemblance, the supernatural activity, the convenient mystery that requires both your skills and his—doesn't any of this seem too perfect to be real?"

Nora rolled her eyes. "So he looks like his great-great-grandfather. It's genetics. That's all. Apparently, good looks run in the family."

With a glint in her eye, Caroline said, "Well, he's got good genes. I'll give him that."

Caroline closed the locket and set it down gently. "So it looks like you've found the inspiration for your art that you were looking for—and some romance."

"So be happy for me."

"I want to be. And I will be—when I'm sure he's the right man for you. Until then, he'll have to prove himself worthy."

Hearing Nora exhale wearily, Caroline added, "I know. I'm a pain in the ass, but I care about you."

Nora heaved another sigh, this one full of exasperation. "What will it take to convince you that I'm happy?"

"Oh, I believe that you're happy. It's just … I have questions."

"I'm afraid to ask."

"Is his research actually credible or just an obsession that's cost him his engagement and his career? And what happens when the mystery is solved and you don't have this project to bond over anymore?" Caroline sat back down, her voice gentle but relentless. "And would he be interested in you at all if you weren't living in his ancestor's house with a chest full of convenient research material?"

The words hit Nora like physical blows. She'd been so caught up in the romance of their partnership and the thrill of shared discovery that she hadn't considered the valid points in Caroline's questions. Part of her was angry with Caroline for raising so many doubts. But the other part couldn't disagree. What did she really know about Maddox beyond what he'd chosen to tell her?

"You're asking me to doubt everything," Nora said quietly.

"I'm asking you to protect yourself. You left New York because you wanted to live life on your terms, remember? Make sure this isn't just a frying pan-fire situation."

As if responding to the emotional tension in the room, the compass began to spin again, its needle whirling frantically. This time, Caroline watched with dismay, as if it merely confirmed her worst fears.

"The house doesn't like it when I question the fairy tale," she said dryly.

"It's not a fairy tale."

"Isn't it? A beautiful woman moves to a mysterious house, finds a tragic love story from the past, and meets a brooding descendant who needs her help solving the mystery. All you're missing is a ball gown and a glass slipper. And maybe a twinkly tiara."

Nora wanted to argue, but Caroline's words had planted seeds of doubt that were already taking root. What if she was projecting her own desires onto the situation? What if Maddox's interest in her was purely practical, or worse— manipulative? What if she was just the latest in a series of women who'd gotten swept up in his romantic quest?

"I need some air," Nora said, standing abruptly.

"Nora—"

"No, you're right. I need to think about this." She headed toward the door, then turned back. "But Caroline? What if you're wrong? What if sometimes the fairy tale is real?"

Caroline's expression softened with sympathy. "Then I'll dance at your wedding and name my firstborn after you. But please, just … be careful. Promise me you won't make any irreversible decisions until you've known him longer than three weeks."

Nora nodded and, desperate to lighten the mood, added, "I'll wait until week four." As she stepped outside onto the porch, the burden of Caroline's doubts settled over her. She wondered whether she had, indeed, made a terrible mistake.

The harbor view that usually soothed her now seemed to mock her uncertainty. Was Caroline right? Had she been so desperate to find her place in the world that she'd convinced herself this was it—based on a few weeks of coincidences and chemistry?

She sank into one of the wicker chairs on the porch and tried to think objectively about Maddox. What did she really know about him beyond what he'd told her? That people in town liked him, yes, but small towns could be insular, protective of their own even when they shouldn't be. He was passionate about his research, but passion could cross a line. Hadn't Miranda left him for exactly that reason?

And the resemblance to Elias … Caroline was right. It was almost too perfect to be believed. What were the odds that she'd find artifacts belonging to a man who looked exactly like the historian researching his story? This could all be some elaborate ruse.

A text from Maddox buzzed on her phone. I found some interesting Shaw family records at the historical society. Can't wait to show you. Maybe tomorrow sometime?

The message, which would have thrilled her yesterday, now left her loaded with doubt. Was he really interested in her, or just in what she could provide for his research? Would he have given her a second glance if she'd been renting a cottage on the other side of town instead of living in Elias's house with a basement full of convenient evidence?

"Doubting everything already?" Caroline's voice came from behind her. "I didn't mean to completely destroy your confidence."

"Yes, you did." Nora didn't turn around. "That's exactly what you meant to do."

"Okay, maybe I did." Caroline settled into the chair beside her. "But only because I love you, and I've watched you be too careful with your heart for three years. I don't want to see you swing too far in the other direction."

"What if I want to swing too far in the other direction? What if I'm tired of being careful?"

"Then I'll support you. But I'll also keep asking uncomfortable questions, because that's what friends do."

They sat in silence for a moment, watching a fishing boat navigate toward the harbor. The afternoon light was starting to change, taking on the golden quality that made everything look like a painting.

"He might be what he seems," Caroline said finally. "Kind, honest, and interested in you for you. The coincidences might be just that—coincidences. The supernatural stuff might be …" She gestured vaguely. "I don't know, old house quirks."

"But?"

"But you've known him for a few weeks, and you're already rearranging your life around his mission." Caroline turned to face her. "Just promise me you won't lose yourself in his story. Whatever this is—research partnership, romance, cosmic destiny—make sure you're still Nora at the center of it."

"I promise," Nora said, and this time she meant it.

"Good." Caroline stood and stretched. "Now, I'm starving, and I refuse to spend my entire Maine vacation analyzing your love life. Where's the best place to get lobster around here?"

Despite everything, Nora smiled. "There's a place called Salty's that Maddox showed me yesterday. The lobster rolls are incredible."

"Perfect. You can tell me more about this town, and I can tell you about the latest drama at my agency. Deal?"

"Deal."

As they headed inside to get ready for dinner, Nora felt some of the tension ease from her shoulders. Caroline's questions had been hard to hear, but maybe that was exactly what she'd needed. A reminder to stay grounded, to keep asking questions, and to make sure she was living her best life instead of getting swept away by someone else's.

But as she grabbed her jacket from the hook by the door, her gaze fell on the artifacts still arranged on the coffee table.

Whatever doubts Caroline had raised, whatever cautions she needed to heed, Nora couldn't shake the feeling that she belonged here. The house, the mystery, even Maddox—they all felt like pieces of a puzzle she was meant to solve.

She just needed to make sure she didn't lose herself in the process.

As they left for dinner, neither woman noticed the locket fall open on the coffee table, revealing Elias's portrait watching the empty room with eyes that seemed almost alive in the changing light.

CHAPTER SEVEN

THE SOUND of Caroline's rental car fading down Mariner's Bluff left Nora standing alone on her front porch, feeling oddly bereft. Her best friend's parting words still echoed in her mind: "Just promise me you won't lose yourself in someone else's story."

Inside, she walked past the artifacts on her coffee table —Elias's compass, the logbook, the locket with his portrait —feeling as though she were neglecting them. After climbing the stairs to her studio, she set up a blank canvas on her easel, squeezed paint onto her palette, and then ... stopped. Caroline's concerns played on repeat in her mind. Was she really here for her art, or was she just another woman getting swept up in Maddox's romantic quest?

Her phone buzzed with a text from Maddox: Hilda said we can come by at 10 to go through more Shaw family papers. Interested?

Nora stared at the message, her thumb hovering over the keyboard. Yesterday, she would have responded imme-diately with enthusiasm. Today, everything felt complicated. She typed and deleted several responses before settling on: *See you then*.

The reply felt cold and distant. She immediately regretted both the brevity and the acceptance. Every decision she made now was mired in doubt.

The walk to town gave her time to think, though her thoughts kept circling back to the same uncomfortable questions. Three days ago, she'd been certain she was following her artistic instincts to Maine. Now she wondered if she'd just been running toward a romantic fantasy, as Caroline suspected.

She passed Mrs. Foster walking her arthritic golden retriever, and the older woman waved cheerfully. "How are you settling in, dear?"

"Very well, thank you," Nora replied, surprised by how much she meant it. Despite her doubts about Maddox, and Caroline's warnings, she did feel like she belonged here in a way she'd never felt in Manhattan.

The historical society occupied a converted Victorian house on Main Street, its rooms filled with glass cases of maritime artifacts and faded photographs of long-dead fishermen. Maddox was waiting at a wooden table in the research room, several archival boxes arranged before him. He looked up when she entered, and she caught a flicker of uncertainty in his eyes.

"Morning," he said in a neutral tone.

"Good morning." She took the chair across from him, acutely aware of the space between them. Yesterday they would have sat side by side, shoulders brushing as they worked. Today felt like a negotiation.

"How did the rest of Caroline's visit go?" he asked, pulling out a folder of documents.

"Fine. She left this morning to continue her coastal

tour." Nora left out her friend's pointed questions about romantic fantasies and the warning about losing herself.

They worked through the Shaw family papers with methodical care. Birth certificates, property deeds, household accounts—the ordinary detritus of lives lived and lost. There was more evidence of the family's decline after the shipwreck: unpaid bills, a notice from the bank, Martha Shaw's increasingly erratic handwriting in her household ledger.

"Look at this," Maddox said, sliding a document across the table. It was a doctor's bill from October 1871, just weeks after the shipwreck. The itemized charges included multiple visits and "medicinal spirits for nervous complaints."

"Martha was falling apart," Nora observed, studying the shaky signature on the payment record.

"Guilt can do that to a person." Maddox sounded matter-of-fact, but Nora heard the underlying excitement. This was more evidence supporting a theory that Marhta was somehow involved. It was one more piece in a puzzle he'd been trying to solve for years.

Nora studied his face as he worked, noting the way his eyes brightened as he handled each piece of paper as if it were precious. She recognized the same kind of passion that drove her to capture light on canvas or express emotion through color.

They worked with painstaking courtesy, but Nora stole glances at him as he read, at the way his brow furrowed in concentration, and the unconscious way he worried his lower lip when he was thinking. When he leaned closer to show her a document, the warmth of his body and the clean scent of his skin made it impossible to focus on the page. She lost all concentration and instead wondered what it would feel like to trace the strong line of his jaw or to thread her fingers through his dark hair.

The awareness seemed to be mutual. She caught him watching her with an intensity that had nothing to do with their research, his gaze lingering on her mouth when she spoke or the way her hair fell across her shoulder when she bent over a document. The space between them seemed to crackle with chemistry, making even the simple act of passing papers feel charged with meaning.

When they'd exhausted the contents of the boxes, Maddox began repacking the documents.

"I should get back," Nora said, standing. "Thank you for including me in this."

"Of course." He looked like he wanted to say something else, but instead, he just nodded. "I'll let you know if I find anything else."

The walk home felt longer than the walk into town. Her thoughts strayed to the miniature portrait of Mabel she'd photographed yesterday—that radiant young woman with hope shining in her painted eyes. By the time she reached her front door, she knew what she needed to do.

Back in her studio, Nora was pulling out her phone to look at the lighthouse museum photos when it rang. The caller ID showed her agent's name, Paisley Crawford.

"Nora!" Paisley's voice bubbled with excitement. "I've got the most incredible opportunity for you. Remember that lifestyle brand I mentioned a few months ago? Hearts at Home? They've got the TV show, the magazine, the retail stores—"

"The one with the farmhouse aesthetic?" Nora sank into the chair by her easel, already knowing where this was heading.

"Exactly! Well, they're expanding into coastal collections, and they want you to be their signature artist. Think about it—Nora Delaney Designs for Hearts at Home. Your work on throw pillows, wall art, dinnerware, even fabric lines."

Nora looked around her studio, at the harbor view, and at the blank canvas waiting on her easel.

"It gets even better," Paisley continued. "They've got partnerships lined up. We're talking about one of the biggest home goods retailers in the country for mass distribution, plus a major home improvement network wants to do a tie-in show. 'Coastal Living with Nora Delaney' or something like that. This could make you a household name."

"It's a three-year exclusive contract," Paisley added. "Seven figures, Nora. Plus royalties. Plus the exposure would set you up for life. They specifically mentioned wanting 'authentic New England charm.' Your move to Maine couldn't have been more perfectly timed. They want someone who actually lives the coastal lifestyle, not just paints it. Of course your time would be divided between the two locations."

Nora stared at the photos of Mabel's miniature on her phone—the young woman's face glowing with joy for the life she had laid out before her. Then she looked at her easel, where she was about to paint the true story of that love and hope, and the tragedy that followed.

"Paisley," she said quietly, "this is incredible, but I need to think about it. Can I call you back in a few days?"

"A few days? Nora, this is Hearts at Home. They're not going to wait around—they have other artists ready to step up to the plate."

"I understand. I just need time to figure out if this is really what I want."

"What's to figure out? This is everything you've been working toward."

After Paisley hung up, Nora sat staring at the contract. Seven figures. National exposure. Everything she'd thought she wanted all those years when she struggled in New York. But now, looking out at the harbor where fishing boats were heading out for their afternoon runs, all she could think about was her new life here. She had finally arrived at the place she'd always longed to be, by the sea painting from her heart and not for her purse.

And then there was Maddox. Of course, they'd just met. She could not make a decision based on a man she barely knew. But he was part of this place, this community she already loved, and he was a man she could love if given the chance. But was that chance worth turning down the opportunity of a lifetime?

She needed to paint. That had always been her coping mechanism. The world could be falling down around her, but art helped her rise above it.

Once settled at her easel, she looked out at the harbor and wondered how often Mabel might have stood in that same spot and looked out as she'd pondered her own situation. Nora set her phone aside and scrolled through the photos she'd taken at the lighthouse museum. It was hard to imagine the woman in the miniature portrait was once a living, breathing woman who had loved and lost in this very house. This wild coast had so many stories to tell, and she wanted to paint them all.

But would Hearts at Home want that story? Would they want the tragedy and complexity of what had happened here, or would they want a cozy, commercialized version of coastal living that could be mass-produced and sold to suburban customers who'd never lived by the ocean?

Nora set up a larger canvas and began to sketch. Not copying the miniature exactly, but expanding it, imagining Mabel in her daily life. She placed her in the front parlor of this very house, sitting in a chair by the window that looked out at the harbor. In Nora's vision, Mabel held a letter—perhaps one of Elias's messages from his final voyage—and her face carried that same hopeful expression from the miniature.

As she worked, something changed inside Nora. This wasn't about supporting Maddox's research or proving Caroline wrong about romantic fantasies. This was about giving voice to a woman history had forgotten, one woman of many who had lived rich lives that mattered. Nora longed to tell Mabel's story and the other stories of people who'd lived by the sea. Nora burned with the familiar fire of creative purpose, a fire she thought had gone out years ago.

The painting flowed from her brush with a passionate ease she hadn't felt since her art school days, before commercial deadlines and client demands slowly drained the joy from her work. This was what she'd come to Maine to find—not to escape from her problems, but to free her true artistic vision to tell stories that mattered. Paisley wanted her to paint "authentic coastal living," but what Nora was painting was authentically coastal and true to her heart for the first time in her career.

As the late afternoon light lingered, the oppressive feeling she'd carried since Caroline's visit was completely gone. She stepped back from her easel. The painting was still rough and unfinished, but already she could see its power. Mabel was coming to life on the canvas, radiantly human. This wasn't the tragic victim of Maddox's historical account. This was a woman full of love as she waited for her husband to come home.

Nora studied her work with growing satisfaction. This was just the beginning. She could envision a whole series with Mabel and Elias's love story told through her art—the wedding day, the last goodbye before his final voyage, perhaps even the terrible night when the storm struck and the lighthouse went dark. She could bring their humanity to life in a way that dry historical records never could.

Brush in hand, Nora felt like herself—not the commercial artist painting cheerful teacup floral designs or the lonely woman who'd bought a house sight unseen in search of a romantic ideal of a life by the sea. She was an artist with something important to say.

Her phone sat on the windowsill with Paisley's offer hanging in the balance, but any decision about Hearts at Home would have to wait. This painting and this moment were what mattered right now.

Nora cleaned her brushes and put away her paints as the sun began to set over the harbor. Tomorrow she would continue working, adding layers and details, bringing Mabel fully to life on canvas. And after that, there would be other paintings, other moments in the story that deserved to be remembered and honored.

She wasn't fulfilling someone else's vision or adding to someone's decor. She was expressing what she saw and felt in her heart, one brushstroke at a time.

A breeze brushed past the windows like a satisfied sigh. Nora had found her purpose. The harbor beyond caught the last shimmering light of the day, and Nora smiled. She was home.

CHAPTER EIGHT

THE KNOCK at Nora's door came at six-thirty. She opened it to find Maddox standing on her porch with two large pizza boxes balanced in one hand and a bottle of wine tucked under his other arm.

"When I got your call, I decided it wouldn't do to come empty-handed," he said, his eyes crinkling with amusement. "Plus, I thought we could spread out all my research and see if we missed anything."

"You're a lifesaver," Nora said, stepping aside to let him in. She'd been living on coffee and the occasional piece of toast, too absorbed in her painting to think about proper meals. "What did you get?"

"One pepperoni and one plain. I wasn't sure what you liked, so I went with safe choices."

"Pizza, huh?" Nora raised an eyebrow with a teasing smile. "You realize I'm from New York, right? I've been spoiled by the real thing my entire life, so the bar's set pretty high."

"Well," Maddox said, matching her playful tone, "I think you'll manage well enough with what I brought you.

Tony's has been holding its own against city competition for twenty years."

He set the boxes on her kitchen counter and looked around at the house. "You've made this place feel like home already."

"Thanks. It's not finished, but I got painting, and everything else had to wait."

When they opened the boxes, the aroma that escaped made Nora's mouth water. The crust was perfectly charred around the edges, the cheese was bubbled and golden, and the sauce smelled of garlic and oregano. She took her first bite and paused, surprised.

"Okay," she admitted, "this is really good. New York had better watch out—Tony knows what he's doing."

"Well, that's high praise from a city girl," Maddox said with a grin.

Maddox started spreading his research materials across her coffee table and the surrounding living room floor. File folders, photocopied documents, photographs, and handwritten notes created a papery landscape that somehow made the room feel more alive.

"This is impressive," Nora said, settling cross-legged on the floor beside him with her plate balanced on her knees. "How long have you been collecting all this?"

"Five years, give or take." Maddox opened the wine and poured two glasses. "Sometimes I look at it and think I'm documenting every sneeze and hiccup from 1871. Other times I think I'm missing something obvious."

"Like what?"

"That's the problem—if I knew what, I'd have found it already." He handed her a glass and raised his own. "To having help deciphering all of this."

"To solving 150-year-old mysteries," she replied, touching her glass to his.

They ate and talked, the conversation flowing as easily as the wine. Maddox told her about his academic frustrations and how his colleagues had distanced themselves as his research became more focused on this one case. Nora shared her own stories of artistic compromise and the slow death of creativity under commercial demands.

"The worst part," she said as she folded a second slice in half, "was that I convinced myself I was being practical and responsible—which I was, to a point. But eventually, I realized it was no longer about money. I was just scared to risk failing at something I cared so much about."

"And now?"

"Now I'm terrified, but it's a good kind of terror." She grinned as she gestured toward her studio upstairs. "I'm painting again. Really painting, not just churning out pretty pictures for people who want art that matches their sofas. I started painting Mabel yesterday. I can't remember the last time I felt so connected to my work."

Maddox leaned back against the couch and studied her face in the warm lamplight. "You're different from when I first met you. More settled. Like you've found your footing."

"Maine has done that for me." She took a sip of wine. "Or maybe it's having a purpose beyond myself. This story matters, doesn't it? Elias and Mabel deserve to have the truth told."

"They do." The now familiar self-doubt came to Maddox's eyes. "I just hope I haven't been chasing shadows all this time."

"You haven't. The evidence is there—we just need to piece it together."

They'd been poring over documents for another hour when the lights flickered. Both of them looked up at the overhead fixture as it wavered, then steadied.

"Old house?" Maddox asked.

"Maybe. But Milt updated the electrical." As if summoned by her words, the lights flickered again, more dramatically this time. Through the windows, Nora could see the trees outside beginning to sway. "Or maybe it's the weather."

The wind had picked up while they'd been talking, and now it rattled the windows with increasing intensity. Lightning flickered in the distance, followed several seconds later by a low rumble of thunder.

"The storm's moving in fast," Maddox observed, glancing toward the harbor view. "Maybe I should head out."

The lights went out completely, plunging the room into darkness.

"Well," Nora said after a moment, "that settles that."

They sat in the blackness, listening to the storm intensify outside. Wind howled around the house, and rain began pattering against the windows with increasing force.

"Do you have any candles?" Maddox asked.

"I think I've got some in the kitchen drawer. I'll get them." Nora felt her way across the room, being careful to avoid the research papers scattered on the floor. She groped her way along the wall to the kitchen and fumbled through the drawers until her fingers closed around several pillar candles and a box of matches.

The first match flared to life, casting dancing shadows on the walls as she lit the candles. The warm light transformed the room—what had been a comfortable living space became something more intimate, more romantic. The research papers looked like ancient manuscripts spread across the floor, and Maddox, illuminated by candlelight, looked like he belonged in another century.

"Better," he said, accepting a candle from her as she returned to their makeshift workspace.

"Much." She settled back beside him, acutely aware of how the flickering light made everything feel more intense, more significant. "Though I should probably think about getting a generator if the power goes out regularly."

"Not a bad idea in these parts, especially during storm season." Maddox positioned his candle on the coffee table where it could illuminate the documents. "The lighthouse would have had backup lighting systems, but even those could have failed if—"

He stopped mid-sentence, his whole body going still.

"What?" Nora asked.

"The lighthouse." He stared at the candle flame, then at her, his eyes wide with sudden understanding. "The light going out. That's what we're missing."

"What do you mean?"

Maddox began shuffling through the papers with renewed urgency, his movements sharp and focused. "There was something in the investigation records. A witness statement that got dismissed. Where is it?" He pulled folders toward him, scanning documents by candle-light. "Here—no, not this one. There was a fisherman who lived up on Pine Street …"

"The same street Captain Joe mentioned? Where his great-grandfather lived?"

"Yes!" Maddox's excitement was building. "Wait, let me find it." He continued searching through the papers, muttering to himself. "Thomas … Leighton, Joe's great-grandfather. He gave testimony to the maritime inquiry, but they discounted it because—here!"

He pulled out a photocopied page, holding it close to the candle to read. "'Mr. Leighton stated that he observed the lighthouse beam fail during the storm,'" he read aloud.

"'However, when pressed for details, he admitted the weather conditions made observation difficult, so the apparent light failure could have been caused by storm clouds obscuring his view.' They dismissed him because he couldn't be certain."

"But what if he was right?" Nora leaned closer, trying to read over his shoulder. "What if the light really did go out?"

"That's exactly what I'm thinking." Maddox set down the Leighton testimony and began pulling out more documents. "If one person noticed it, maybe others did too. Let me check the other witness statements."

In the candlelight, they sorted through testimony after testimony. Most witnesses had taken shelter and hadn't seen anything useful. But from those remaining, a pattern began to emerge.

"Look at this," Nora said, pointing to a statement from a woman named Sarah Kelley. "'The lighthouse seemed dark when I looked out my window to check on the storm, but it was hard to tell with all the rain.'"

"And here," Maddox added, his voice rising with excitement. "James Porter testified, 'I couldn't see the light from my house like I usually could, but I figured it must be the weather.' They all mention not seeing the light, but they all attribute it to the storm conditions."

Nora pulled another folder toward her and squinted at a statement they'd skimmed over earlier. "Listen to this one from late afternoon—Ada Daniels: 'I looked out during the worst of it to check if our shutters were holding. I could still make out shapes in the storm, and I saw someone leaving the lighthouse, moving quick over the lawn. I couldn't make out who it was in all that rain and wind, but I know it wasn't Jasper Shaw—this person walked upright and steady. Poor Jasper's back troubles make him hunch over something awful.'"

"Someone leaving the lighthouse," Maddox breathed, leaning closer to read over her shoulder. "During the storm."

"But she couldn't see who it was," Nora said, then paused. "No one could."

"What do you mean?"

"The people in the witness statements. They all say they couldn't see clearly because of the darkness and the weather." Nora's excitement was building. "But they all consistently mention the same thing—they couldn't see the lighthouse beam."

Maddox stared at her, and then at the scattered papers. "Because there wasn't one to see."

"Exactly. Even in terrible weather, you'd be able to make out some trace of a lighthouse beam. It might be diffused by the rain or fog, but wouldn't you see something? But for multiple witnesses to see nothing ..."

"The light wasn't just obscured," Maddox finished. "It was out. Completely out."

Their eyes met as they grasped the significance. If the lighthouse beam had been completely extinguished rather than just difficult to see through the storm, that changed everything.

"So why would the light go out?" Nora mused. "The official inspection found no mechanical problems."

"The equipment was fine," Maddox agreed, flipping through the maritime inquiry records. "There was no damage to the lamp mechanism, no structural issues with the lighthouse itself."

"So either there was some kind of failure they couldn't detect or ..." Nora trailed off as she studied the witness statements again.

Maddox said, "Or someone deliberately shut off the light."

The words hung between them in the flickering candlelight.

Nora whispered, "But that would mean ..."

"That someone wanted that ship to crash." Maddox pulled Thomas Leighton's testimony back toward him, reading it with new eyes. "Leighton said he saw someone leaving the lighthouse during the storm. But if it wasn't Jasper Shaw checking the light ..."

Nora nodded and reached for one of the papers. "Which it wasn't, because Jasper's back troubles made him hunch over, and 'this person walked upright and steady.' So, Jasper Shaw didn't let the light go out. Someone else put it out. And whoever it was, Leighton saw him."

The implications hung between them in the candlelit room. Outside, the storm raged on, wind and rain battering the house in a way that made it easy to imagine that terrible night in 1871.

"Which means it couldn't have been Shaw's negligence," Nora said quietly. "It was someone's direct fault."

"Exactly."

"Then Elias wasn't reckless or incompetent. He was trying to navigate in conditions where the one thing he was counting on—the lighthouse beam—wasn't there."

They looked at each other across the candle-lit papers, both grasping the magnitude of what they might have discovered. It wasn't proof yet, but it was the first real evidence that the official story might be wrong.

"Maddox," Nora said in hushed tones, "I think we've got something here."

"I think we do too." His eyes were bright with excitement and hope. "After five years of everyone telling me I was chasing ghosts ..."

They'd found it—not the complete answer, but the thread that might lead them there.

Without thinking, Nora launched herself forward and threw her arms around Maddox's neck. He caught her instinctively, his arms closing around her waist as she held him tight.

"We did it," she breathed against his ear. "We actually found something real."

"We did," he said, his voice rough with emotion.

The atmosphere was electric. In the flickering candlelight, with rain lashing the windows, the rest of the world felt far away. They were alone. It was overpowering, this attraction that had been building since that first night when he'd appeared on her doorstep. And now, her heart raced with desire to taste the wine on his lips.

His arms tightened around her, and for a moment, they held each other in the soft candlelight and shared the pure joy of discovery.

But then awareness crept in—the warmth of his body against hers, the clean scent of his skin, the way her heart was racing for reasons that had nothing to do with historical research. She became acutely conscious of how close they were, how natural it felt to be in his arms.

She pulled back, her cheeks burning. "I'm … sorry. I just got excited about—"

"No, it's …" Maddox's hands lingered on her waist for a heartbeat before he let them drop. "It's okay."

Thunder crashed overhead and made them both jump. With that, the spell broke—but the awareness remained, humming between them like a live wire.

In the flickering light, their eyes met, filled with more than the thrill of discovery. The research papers scattered around them seemed forgotten as they navigated this new awareness of each other.

"So," Nora said finally, clearing her throat and gesturing toward the documents. "What's our next step?"

"Right. Next step." Maddox ran a hand through his hair, clearly trying to refocus. "We need more evidence. This is suggestive, but not conclusive. We need to find out more about the lighthouse keeper—Jasper Shaw. His personal records, his state of mind, anything that might explain why the light would have gone out."

"Where would we find that kind of information?"

"Family records, maybe. Personal papers. The historical society might have more Shaw family materials." He began gathering the witness statements together. "Or we might get lucky at an estate sale or auction. Sometimes family documents surface decades later when houses get cleaned out."

"It's a start," Nora agreed. "At least now we know what we're looking for."

"We do." Maddox's voice was quiet, thoughtful. "Nora?"

"Yeah?"

"Thank you. For believing in this. For helping me see things I missed. I couldn't have found this connection without you."

"You would have eventually. You're too thorough not to have spotted the pattern."

"Maybe." He stood and began stacking his papers. "I should let you get some sleep. It's getting late, and the storm doesn't seem to be letting up."

"Are you sure you should drive in this weather?" Nora glanced toward the windows, where rain was still lashing against the glass.

"I'll be fine. It's not far to my place." But he hesitated, and she wondered if he was reluctant to leave for the same reasons she was reluctant to have him go.

The evening had changed things between them. They'd crossed a line from research partners to something more personal, something that made her pulse race and her skin feel too warm.

"Drive carefully," she said, walking him to the door.

"I will." He paused on the threshold, looking back at her in the candlelight. "Tomorrow we start digging into Jasper Shaw's life. See what secrets he might have been hiding."

"Tomorrow," she agreed.

After he left, Nora stood at the front window watching his taillights disappear down Mariner's Bluff. The storm was beginning to subside, but her heart was still racing from more than just their discovery.

They'd found their first real clue. But more than that, they'd found something else—a connection that went deeper than shared purpose. The question was whether they were brave enough to explore it, or if they'd let fear of complicating their relationship keep them at arm's length.

As she blew out the last candle and headed upstairs in the darkness, Nora suspected that particular question would be much harder to answer than any 150-year-old mystery.

CHAPTER NINE

NORA WAS on her way to the kitchen when she heard a knock. Not the confident rap from earlier in the evening, but something more hesitant, almost apologetic. She opened the door to find Maddox standing on her porch again, his hair damp from the rain that was still falling steadily.

"I'm sorry to bother you again," he said, running a hand through his wet hair. "But there's a tree down across Harbor Road, and another one blocking the turn onto Pine Street. I'm basically trapped until the road crew can get out there in the morning."

"Oh no." Nora stepped aside without hesitation. "Come in, you're soaking wet."

He hesitated on the threshold. "I'm sorry. I hate to ask, but would you mind if I crash on your couch? Or I could sleep in my car if—"

"Don't be ridiculous. I'll go get a pillow and blanket." She closed the door behind him. "Besides, after the breakthrough we had tonight, I'm too wired to sleep, anyway. Want some wine? I'll go get a bottle."

Relief flickered across his face. "That sounds perfect."

Nora got the wine from the kitchen and left Maddox to open it while she went upstairs for a blanket and pillow.

He'd only left minutes before, but the atmosphere felt different now. More intimate. Having Maddox stranded here by the storm made the house feel like a refuge cut off from the rest of the world.

"There." She set the blanket and pillow on a chair, and then settled onto the couch across from Maddox, tucking her legs under her. "So, are the road crews pretty quick around here?"

"They do a good job. Our winters give them plenty of practice. Fingers crossed, I'll be out of here by noon." Maddox leaned against the arm of the sofa and faced Nora. "I hope you don't mind the company."

"Are you kidding? After what we found tonight, I'm glad you're here to talk to, or I'd be up all night thinking about it." She took a sip of wine and studied his face in the candlelight.

Maddox was quiet, swirling the wine in his glass. "I don't know why I didn't make the connection before." He paused, his eyes focused on the rain streaming down the windows. "I've been having this dream," he said finally. "It didn't make any sense until tonight."

Nora waited, eager to hear more.

"It's about that night—the shipwreck. I'm on the deck of the *Steadfast*, and I can see the lighthouse beam sweeping across the water, guiding us home. But then it just … goes out. Complete darkness when I need it most."

"When did the dreams start?"

"The night the pocket watch began working again. At first, I thought it was just the stress of losing my job, having my book rejected, and getting nowhere with my research. I figured it was getting to me. But since we found those witness statements …" He looked up at her. "I don't know. It just fell into place. The lighthouse goes dark. And it feels so real, like I'm actually there."

Nora felt a chill. "Like you're experiencing what Elias experienced."

"Exactly. The light goes out, and I hear this loud crack. The ship splits apart, and I'm swallowed by the sea. And then I wake up gasping for air."

Nora said, "Maddox! That's not a dream—it's a nightmare."

Maddox nodded. "I know. And I can't prove a case with a dream, but I know that I'm right. Something happened that night. The light was deliberately extinguished, and the truth of it never came out." He leaned forward, his intensity palpable even in the soft candlelight. "And … I sound a little insane."

"No," she said quietly. "You don't. You sound like your subconscious has processed everything you've been learning. And it's just now coming to the surface. You're making connections you weren't consciously aware of yet."

"Or I'm losing my grip on reality. No harm there. Everyone thinks I've lost it already."

She was moved by the pain in his voice. "Who's everyone?"

"My colleagues. My family. Miranda." He took a long sip of wine. "She's engaged to a cardiologist who, according to my mother, is charming and doesn't spend every conversation talking about dead relatives."

"Ouch."

"The thing is, I have been obsessed with this. I've let it consume my career, my relationships, probably my mental stability." He looked directly at her. "But I can't let it go, Nora. Not when I'm this close to the truth."

"Why is it so important to you? I mean, beyond the historical significance?"

Maddox was quiet for so long she thought he wasn't going to answer. When he finally spoke, it was barely above a whisper.

"Because everyone thinks Elias was a failure. That he made a stupid, reckless decision that cost seven men their lives. That's his legacy—Captain Wheeler, the fool who sailed into a storm." He set down his wine glass and stared at his hands. "And sometimes I wonder if that's my legacy too. The descendant who couldn't let sleeping dogs lie, who threw away everything real in his life chasing ghosts."

"But what if you're right? What if Elias was innocent?"

"Then maybe I'm not the obsessed fool everyone thinks I am. Maybe I'm actually fighting for something that matters—like truth." He looked up at her, and the vulnerability in his eyes made her breath catch. "Do you know what it's like to have everyone you care about think you're wasting your life?"

Nora thought about her years in New York, painting roosters and flowers while her real artistic voice withered. About the art school friends who'd stopped inviting her to gallery openings because they thought she'd sold out. About the loneliness that drove her to buy a house sight unseen in a town she'd never visited.

"Actually, I do," she said softly. "For years, I convinced myself I was being practical by painting what sold instead of what I loved. People—my agent, for one—told me I was smart to have a steady income, that I was being realistic about my career. But inside, I felt like I was dying a little more each day."

"What changed?"

"I realized that, in a way, playing it safe was the riskiest thing I could do. I'd rather fail at something I cared about than succeed at something that meant nothing to me." She met his eyes across the flickering candlelight. "Maybe that's what you're doing too."

Something changed in Maddox's expression, a wall coming down that she hadn't even realized was there. "I haven't had anyone believe in me for a very long time."

"Well, you do now."

They sat in silence as the storm raged outside and the candles cast dancing shadows on the walls. Nora studied his face—the strong jawline, the way his dark hair caught the light, the intensity in his eyes that reminded her so much of the portrait in Elias's locket.

"Can I ask you something?" she said. "What was your life like before all this? Before the research took over?"

"Boring," he said with a self-deprecating smile. "I taught maritime history at Rockland, published papers that nobody read, and went to faculty mixers where everyone complained about their tenure track prospects." He paused. "I was with Miranda for a year, and honestly, I think we were both just going through the motions. She wanted stability, and I wanted … I don't know. Something more than what I had."

"And now?"

"Now I'm unemployed, single, and camping out in the family's vacation cottage while I chase a 150-year-old mystery." He laughed, but there was something lighter in it now. "Somehow, though, this feels more real than anything I've done in years."

"I know what you mean."

Maddox said softly, "When's the last time you felt truly present in your own life, Nora? Not going through the motions, not playing a role you think you should play, but actually living?"

The question hit her harder than she'd expected. "Before

now? Probably not since art school." She pulled her knees up to her chest, wrapping her arms around them. "I spent so many years trying to be the person everyone expected me to be that I forgot who I really was underneath it all."

"And now?"

"Now I'm sitting in a room with a man I met a few weeks ago, investigating a century-old mystery, and it feels like the most honest thing I've ever done." She smiled. "Of course, my best friend thinks I've lost my mind."

"Maybe we both have. But maybe that's not such a bad thing."

Their eyes met, and everything seemed to go still, then they both began talking at once and stopped just as quickly. With a weak smile, Maddox said, "We should probably ..." he started, but his words trailed off.

"Yeah," she agreed, though she made no move to put more distance between them.

A tremendous crack of thunder shook the house, followed by what sounded like another tree falling somewhere nearby. They both jumped. With a curse, Nora clutched Maddox's arm.

He put a steady hand on her shoulder. "That was close."

"Too close." Nora's heart pounded.

They sat there for another moment as thunder rolled away into the distance, but the electricity in the air remained.

"I'm sorry. I'm keeping you up," Maddox said finally, though his voice lacked conviction.

"No, you're not." Instead of getting up, Nora settled back into the corner of the couch, pulling a throw pillow into her lap. "I'm still too wired to sleep."

They talked for another hour, their conversation ranging from the mystery to their childhoods to their dreams for the future. The wine and the late hour made them both more open, more honest than they might have been otherwise. Gradually, their positions on the couch became more relaxed, more comfortable.

Nora was on her side with her head propped on her hand, while on his side, Maddox stretched his long legs out on the coffee table, his feet nearly touching hers. The candles burned lower, casting gentler shadows, and the storm outside began to subside into steady rain.

Sometime after midnight, Nora said, "I should let you get some sleep."

"Or we could stay here for a while," Maddox said, his eyes heavy with wine and exhaustion.

So neither of them moved. The house was warm and comfortable, and somehow it felt natural to stay where they were, safe and right.

Their wine glasses sat forgotten on the coffee table, and the research papers scattered on the floor seemed like artifacts from another world. All that mattered was this moment, this conversation, this connection that felt deeper than anything she'd experienced in years.

"Can I tell you something?" Maddox said softly.

"Anything."

"That first night when I knocked on your door, I was ready to give up. On the research, on everything. I'd convinced myself that everyone was right, that I was chasing ghosts." He looked directly at her. "But then you believed me. Without question, without hesitation. Do you have any idea what that meant?"

"But you would have figured it out. You're too thorough, too dedicated to—"

"No." He shook his head. "I was done. Completely done. But you saw something in the story that I'd stopped seeing. You reminded me why it mattered." His hand moved as if to reach for hers, then stopped. "You made me feel like I mattered."

The space between them felt charged, electric. Nora was acutely aware of how close they were sitting, of the way the candlelight made his eyes look almost silver, and of the fact that she wanted to close the distance between them more than she'd wanted anything in a very long time.

"Maddox," she said, in nearly a whisper.

"I know." His voice was rough. "We just met. This is ... soon, I know—"

"I don't care." The words came out before she could stop them. "About timing, about any of it."

They looked at each other in the flickering light, both balanced on the edge of something that would change everything. The storm outside seemed to fade away, leaving only the soft glow of candlelight and the sound of their breathing.

Maddox lifted his hand and gently touched her face, his thumb tracing her cheekbone. "Are you sure?"

Instead of answering, Nora leaned into his touch and closed her eyes for a moment. When she opened them again, his face was closer, and she could see the question in his eyes—the hope mixed with uncertainty.

She answered by closing the final distance between them, her lips meeting his in a kiss that was soft at first, tentative then deeper, as his arms came around her and pulled her closer. The taste of wine lingered between them, and the tension she'd been carrying with her finally released. This was what she'd been missing in New York. In all those practical years, she'd never felt so at home with anyone as she did with Maddox. She didn't care that they'd only just met. She just cared about how she felt in his arms and the feel of his lips against hers. She just cared about him.

When they finally parted, Maddox rested his forehead against hers. "I've wanted to do that since you first opened your door," he admitted.

Nora laughed softly. "Just since then?"

"I knew right then I was in trouble."

They stayed close, in an unspoken understanding that something fundamental had changed between them. Outside, the storm continued to rage, but inside they'd found something worth sheltering.

Nora's eyes drifted closed as she listened to the rain against the windows and the soft sound of Maddox's breathing. The last thing she remembered was feeling more utterly content than she had in years.

NORA WOKE to pale morning light from the windows. She was lying on her side, but now her head was pillowed on his shoulder, and their legs were tangled together beneath the throw blanket someone, probably Maddox, had pulled over them both.

For a moment, she simply lay there, listening to his steady breathing, acutely aware of the warmth of his body and the clean scent of his skin. This was dangerous territory —waking up in someone's arms after knowing them for less than a month. But it felt so natural, so right, that she couldn't bring herself to regret it.

Maddox stirred beside her, and she felt the moment he became aware of where he was. His body tensed slightly, then relaxed.

"Good morning," he said softly, his voice rough with sleep.

"Morning." She didn't move away, not yet. "Sleep well?"

"For the most part." His arm tightened around her almost imperceptibly. "You?"

"Same." She finally lifted her head to look at him, noting the way his hair was mussed and how the morning light made his eyes look lighter. "Any interesting dreams?"

His expression grew more serious. "Actually, yes. The same one, but … different this time."

"Different how?"

"I was still on the ship, still approaching the harbor in the storm. But this time, when the lighthouse went dark, I could see someone in the dim light from the lighthouse window. Just a shadow, but definitely a person." He sat up slightly, his attention fully focused now. "And he wasn't trying to fix the light. He was just … standing there. Watching."

A chill ran down Nora's spine. "Watching the ship approach the rocks?"

"That's how it felt. Like he was waiting to see what would happen." Maddox ran a hand through his hair, fully awake now. "I know it's just a dream, but …"

"But it felt real."

He looked at her intently. "I'm more convinced than ever that someone deliberately let the light go out."

The possibility hung between them, darker and more disturbing than simple negligence. "But we know that it couldn't have been Jasper Shaw."

Maddox furrowed his eyebrows. "But do we? What if the person seen walking away only witnessed the light going out?"

Nora nodded. "Or forced Shaw to do it."

Maddox shook his head slowly. "So who did it? And who was that person who left the lighthouse?"

"And why?" Nora asked, though part of her was

already wondering if they were about to uncover something much worse than they'd bargained for.

"I don't know. But I think it's time we found out everything we can about Shaw and the lighthouse and, for that matter, anyone connected to Jasper Shaw's life in 1871—his finances, his relationships, and his state of mind." Maddox sat up fully now, the investigation taking precedence over the intimacy of their morning wake-up.

Nora sat up as well, acutely aware that they'd crossed back into research partner territory. Their intimacy last night felt like it belonged to a different world, though the memory of it lingered between them like an unfinished conversation.

"Where do we start?" she asked.

"Estate sales. Church records. Maybe the historical society has more lighthouse and Shaw family materials they haven't cataloged yet." He was in full historian mode now. "If someone caused that wreck, someone in his family or a friend might have known about it and written something down."

"Or hidden something away," Nora added, thinking about her own discovery of Elias's artifacts in the basement.

"Exactly." Maddox stood and began gathering up the research papers from the night before. "This changes everything, Nora. If we can prove deliberate sabotage …"

"We clear Elias's name completely."

"And potentially solve one of Maine's oldest maritime mysteries." He paused in his paper-gathering to look at her. "Are you ready for this to get more serious? Because if Shaw deliberately caused that wreck, this isn't just historical research anymore. It's a murder investigation that's 150 years overdue."

Nora looked around her living room at the candles that had burned down to stubs, the wine glasses on the coffee table, and the blanket they'd shared through the night. A month ago, she'd been a commercial artist from New York with no deeper purpose than painting and adding to her investment account. Now she was potentially investigating a century-old murder with a man who was becoming far more important to her than was probably wise.

"I'm ready," she said, and meant it completely.

Outside, she could hear the distant sound of chainsaws as the road crews began clearing the fallen trees. Soon Maddox would be able to leave, and they'd both return to their separate lives. But something fundamental had shifted between them during their night together—not just the kiss, but the deeper intimacy of shared purpose and mutual trust.

Whatever happened the night of the shipwreck, the truth would come out, because they were determined to find it. For the first time in her adult life, Nora felt like she was exactly where she belonged.

CHAPTER TEN

THE CANVAS in front of Nora remained stubbornly blank, even though she'd been standing in her studio for twenty minutes with a brush in her hand.

Last night kept replaying in her mind—the candlelit discovery, the excitement of finding substantial evidence, and the way Maddox had looked at her across the small space between them. His kiss had left her heart racing and her thoughts scattered.

What was she doing? She answered her own question. Falling for him. Hard. The rational part of her mind—the part that sounded suspiciously like Caroline—kept insisting this was all happening too fast, that she was projecting romantic fantasies onto the first attractive man who'd paid attention to her.

But the way he'd touched her face, the vulnerability in his eyes when he'd talked about needing someone to believe in him ... that hadn't felt like a fantasy. It had felt achingly real.

She finally gave up on the seascape and moved to a fresh canvas, letting her brush find its way. Within minutes, she was painting the scene from last night—two figures hunched over scattered papers by candlelight, their faces intent on discovery. It felt rewarding in a way her commercial work never had. What a luxury it was to act on impulse and capture moments that mattered so deeply to her.

Her phone rang, interrupting her thoughts. Maddox's name appeared on the screen, and her heart swelled the way it did every time she saw it.

"Hi," she answered, trying to sound casual.

"Hi, yourself. I hope I'm not interrupting your painting, but I just got a call from the lighthouse museum. They found something during their restoration work—something I think you'll want to see."

"What kind of something?"

"Hilda wouldn't say much over the phone, just that they discovered an old journal hidden under the floorboards. It might be connected to the lighthouse keeper's family." His excitement was palpable even through the phone. "Could you meet me there in twenty minutes?"

Nora looked at her easel and decided her painting could wait. "I'll be right there," she said.

THE LIGHTHOUSE MUSEUM was a flurry of activity when they arrived. Contractors had cordoned off part of the lighthouse keeper's quarters with plastic sheeting, and the sound of power tools echoed from within. Hilda met them at the entrance, practically vibrating with excitement.

"The contractors had to pull up all the flooring in the lighthouse keeper's quarters—the joists were riddled with dry rot," she explained, leading them through the museum. "Salt air just eats away at everything, you know. But they found something tucked underneath the floorboards. A small journal, wrapped in oilcloth."

She led them to a back room where the journal lay on a clean white cloth. The leather binding was dark with age but remarkably intact.

"I've only glanced through it," Hilda said, "but it appears to belong to Martha Shaw and covers most of 1871. I thought you might want to examine it properly."

"Could we possibly borrow it for a few days?" Maddox asked, flashing his most charming smile. "I promise we'll take excellent care of it."

Hilda hesitated, clearly torn between protocol and curiosity. Finally, a twinkle appeared in her eyes. "I suppose … well, I wouldn't let just anyone walk out of here with a piece of history like this. But since it's you … Just don't tell anybody, and have it back to me by the end of the week."

AN HOUR LATER, they were sitting at Maddox's kitchen table with two cups of coffee and the journal between them. Maddox's cottage was exactly what Nora had expected— cozy and masculine, with built-in bookshelves covering every available wall space and maritime artifacts scattered throughout. A ship's compass served as a paperweight on his desk, and an antique sextant held a place of honor on the mantelpiece.

"You do the honors," Nora said, her voice tight with anticipation.

Maddox opened the journal, turning to the first entry. Martha Shaw's daily life unfolded before them in careful script—domestic details that painted a picture of a practical woman dealing with the challenges of coastal life in 1871.

They took turns reading aloud, occasionally chuckling at Martha's observations about her neighbors and her running commentary on daily struggles. The woman who emerged from these pages was devout, practical, and possessed of a dry wit that made even mundane tasks entertaining.

"She mentions Jasper drinking as early as July," Maddox noted, pointing to an entry about him missing the Independence Day celebration due to a mysterious "stomach ailment" that coincided with her finding an empty rum bottle.

As they approached October, the tone of the entries began to change. Martha's concern about her husband's behavior grew more pronounced—his strange moods, increased drinking, and cryptic comments about debts and obligations.

The entry for October 3rd, the night of the shipwreck, was frustratingly brief:

> *Terrible storm. Jasper worked through the night. A ship was lost. Seven souls gone to their rest. God have mercy.*

They continued reading, and the entries that followed painted a devastating picture of the investigation's aftermath.

"October 15, 1871," Nora read aloud.

> *The inquiry men came again today. Poor Jasper, his hands shook so badly he could barely hold his teacup. They examined every inch of the lighthouse mechanism and asked him to walk through that terrible night hour by hour. When they left, he sat in his chair and wept. I have never seen him weep.*

"October 22, 1871," Maddox continued.

The official word came today. The investigators found no fault with Jasper's conduct. The lamp mechanism shows no damage, they said. Simply one of those inexplicable failures that happen in severe weather. Jasper should be relieved, but he only drinks more. "I should have checked again," he keeps saying. Nothing I say helps. Whatever his troubles with drink at home, Jasper has never touched a drop while tending the light. "The ships depend on me," he always says. The inquiry men asked about his drinking habits, and I told them what I've told everyone—Jasper may seek comfort in the bottle in our parlor, but never, not once, has he been anything but sober at his post.

"November 3, 1871," Nora read.

I found him at dawn sitting on the rocks below the lighthouse, staring at where the Steadfast went down. He won't accept what the officials told him—that these things happen, that no one is to blame. "Seven men, Martha," he said. "Seven men dead on my watch." How do I make him understand it wasn't his fault? I know my husband—whatever his failings, he would never drink on duty. Never.

They sat in stunned silence for a moment. "So Shaw was officially cleared," Maddox said quietly. "The investigation found no negligence, no equipment failure they could identify. But he couldn't live with it, anyway. Why?"

"Martha couldn't understand it. He seemed so convinced he'd been negligent."

For several weeks after that, Martha returned to her usual domestic concerns, but her worry about Jasper's declining state peppered the journal until October 28th.

Nora read slowly.

I can bear this no longer. For weeks now I have carried
this burden, and it grows heavier with each passing day. I am
a Christian woman, and I cannot live with this knowledge
without seeking God's forgiveness, even if I cannot seek
man's. Dear Lord, forgive me for what I know and have not
spoken. Jasper came home that terrible night in such a state,
shaking like a leaf and muttering about how he had no choice.
When I pressed him, he looked at me with wild eyes and
said ...

The sentence stopped abruptly. Nora turned the page, but the right side had been torn out, leaving only a jagged edge where the rest of Martha's confession should have been.

"No," Maddox breathed. "No, no, no!"

They both stared at the torn page, the devastating incompleteness of it hitting them like a physical blow.

"She destroyed it," Nora said quietly. "She wrote it down because she couldn't live with the guilt, but then she couldn't live with having written it either."

"But she couldn't bring herself to destroy the whole journal," Maddox added. "So she just tore out the most damning part."

They sat in frustrated silence, staring at the journal that had promised answers but left them with the most important question unresolved.

Maddox closed the journal with a thud and leaned back in his chair, running both hands through his hair. "Five years," he said, sounding hollow. "Five years of chasing leads that go nowhere, of being told I'm obsessed, of watching my career implode. And when we finally find something that could prove everything, it's gone."

"We still have evidence that Jasper was hiding something," Nora offered. "Martha's guilt, his strange behavior, the timing—"

"It's not enough." Maddox stood abruptly and walked to his kitchen counter, pulling out a bottle of wine. "Without that confession, it's still just family folklore and speculation. No publisher—academic or otherwise—will touch it. Hell, no one will believe it."

Nora watched him uncork the wine with sharp, frustrated movements. She could see the disappointment settling over him. All the hope he'd built up was now draining away.

"You know what the worst part is?" he continued, pouring two generous glasses. "For a few hours there, I actually thought I was going to vindicate Elias—clear his name, prove I wasn't some delusional descendant chasing ghosts." He handed her a glass and sank back into his chair. "Maybe Miranda was right. Maybe I should have let this go years ago."

"Don't say that." Nora's voice was fierce. "You were right to keep searching. Elias deserves to have his story told properly."

"Does he? Or am I just projecting my own need for vindication onto a dead man?" Maddox took a long sip of wine. "Maybe the truth is that I've wasted the last five years of my life on something that doesn't matter to anyone but me."

"It matters to me." The words came out more intensely than she'd intended. Maddox looked up, meeting her eyes across the small table.

"Why?" he said softly.

"Because it happened, and the truth is important." She reached across the table and touched his hand. "And you're important. You're not delusional, Maddox. You're passionate about justice. There's a difference."

He turned his hand and grasped hers. "Sometimes I wonder if I used this research as an excuse to avoid living my own life. Miranda used to say I was more comfortable with dead people than living ones."

"Do you really believe that?"

Maddox was quiet for a long moment, his thumb tracing gentle circles on her palm. "I believe that she might have been right. It felt safer to care about people who couldn't disappoint me or decide I wasn't worth the trouble." He looked up at her. "But then you showed up, and …"

"And what?"

"And … I found myself wanting to live in the present. I care about what happens between us." His voice grew softer. "And that scares me."

Nora felt her heart flutter against her ribs. "Why?"

"Because I don't know how to do this. I mean, look at my track record. But I want to see where this is going." He lifted their joined hands, pressing a soft kiss to her knuckles. "Not just the research, but us. I want to see this through with you."

"Good. Because I'm not going anywhere," she said, though the words surprised her with their certainty. Before she'd moved here, she wouldn't have been able to make that promise to anyone. Now it felt like the most honest thing she'd ever said.

"Are you sure?"

Instead of answering with words, she stood and went to him. Maddox met her halfway, and their lips came together with a gentleness that made her heart swell. The kiss was soft, tentative at first, then deeper as he cupped her face with his free hand.

When it ended, he rested his forehead against hers. "I've wanted to do that since the moment you first opened your door." His smile was soft, vulnerable. "You looked so fierce in those sailboat pajamas, like you were ready to take on whatever I was selling. I knew right then I was in trouble."

His words filled her with such warmth that she couldn't help smiling. "You will be in trouble if you give up on this search."

His eyes shone as he took her hands in his. "Then I'd better keep going."

"Good choice."

He drew her into his arms and kissed her until her head swam. When he finally drew back, it was with a deep sigh. "If we don't get back to work now…" The burning look in his eyes was enough to finish his thought. "Maybe some coffee will help motivate us," he said, moving to the counter.

As he prepared it, the rich aroma of brewing coffee filled the kitchen, but there was something else mixed in—a warm, spicy scent that made Nora's breath catch.

"I smell cinnamon," she said, inhaling deeply.

"Sorry, that's all I've got," Maddox said with a sheepish smile.

"No, it's perfect," Nora interrupted, her mind racing. "That scent makes me think about my house. Every time I've looked at that old baking equipment, the vanilla-cinnamon scent gets stronger." Then a serious thought came to mind. "Maddox, what if that's not just a coincidence?"

"What do you mean?"

"I mean, what if Mabel's trying to tell us something? Through her cooking?" Nora stopped herself. "Okay, that sounds like crazy talk."

Maddox's eyes looked intense. "No. Tell me what you were thinking."

Nora hesitated, searching for words. "I just wonder if

we might have been looking at this all wrong. We've been focusing on the lighthouse keeper and the official records, but what about the personal side?"

Maddox looked full of doubt. "Martha's journal? We tried that and see how that turned out."

"Not Martha. Mabel."

Maddox looked confused. "But we've read all her letters. Are you saying we missed something?"

"Not in the letters, but in her daily life. Wouldn't she also have kept household records of some sort? Nineteenth-century women kept journals to record household finances and management, daily activities, personal thoughts, and family events." Nora's excitement was building. "Especially with Elias gone for long periods of time. She was on her own. She might've recorded things Elias had told her, or things she wouldn't want to forget to tell him. There must be a journal."

Maddox stared at her, the implications sinking in. "But has it survived?"

Nora sighed. Maddox was right. It was a big if. But she couldn't just give up. "Okay. Let's back up. We know someone extinguished the lighthouse light."

Maddox winced. "We believe it, but we can't prove it."

"Well, supposing it's true, why would someone do that?"

Maddox narrowed his eyes. "They were targeting someone."

Nora nodded. "Elias."

Maddox frowned. "Not necessarily."

They looked at each other and both realized they might have been investigating the wrong victim entirely.

Nora exhaled, feeling defeated. "Someone else on the ship? But that could have been any number of people."

Maddox rubbed his forehead. "True, but let's start with the people we know, and move on from there."

Nora was overwhelmed by the widening scope of their research.

"We need to go back to your house," Maddox said. "If Mabel left any records, that's where they'd be."

As they gathered their coats and the borrowed Martha Shaw journal, the scent of cinnamon coffee lingered in the air.

CHAPTER ELEVEN

THE DRIVE back to the Captain's Watch felt different from their usual trips between houses. The kiss they'd shared at Maddox's cottage lingered between them, and the cinnamon scent that had filled his kitchen seemed to follow them into the evening air.

"Do you really think she's trying to tell us something?" Maddox asked as they pulled into Nora's driveway. "Or are we just desperate enough to see signs where there aren't any?"

"I know how it sounds," Nora admitted, looking up at the Victorian mansion that had become so much more than just her new home. "But that scent is real. We've both smelled it."

Inside, the vanilla-cinnamon fragrance that had become so familiar was present. But as they moved toward the kitchen, it grew richer and more complex—not just the background scent they'd grown accustomed to, but the smell of baking in progress.

"There," Nora whispered, pointing toward the kitchen. "Do you smell that?"

Maddox nodded, his eyes wide. The scent was unmistakable now—cinnamon rolls rising, butter melting, the warm yeast smell of fresh bread.

They followed the scent into the kitchen, where moonlight from the windows cast everything in silver shadows. The room looked exactly as Nora had left it that morning, but something felt different.

"Look," Maddox said softly, pointing to the counter beside the stove.

There, arranged as if someone had just been using them, were several pieces of vintage baking equipment: a metal pastry cutter with a painted wooden handle, a set of measuring spoons that looked hand-forged, and a small ceramic bowl with delicate blue flowers painted around the rim.

"I don't remember seeing these before," Nora said, approaching the items cautiously. "They must have been tucked away somewhere I missed. But I didn't put them there."

Maddox picked up the pastry cutter, turning it over in his hands. "Look at this craftsmanship. This is definitely 19th century." He paused, studying the handle more closely. "There are initials engraved here: 'M.W.'"

"Mabel Wheeler."

The scent of baking grew stronger, as if responding to their recognition. Nora felt drawn to the cabinet beside the stove where the baking equipment appeared. As she opened it, she spied something in the back behind a stack of her own dishes. In the corner, a small wooden recipe box sat as if it had been waiting for her to find it.

Her hands trembled as she lifted it out. The box was made of the same cedar as the chest she'd found in the basement, and it opened with the same smooth ease despite its obvious age. Inside, dozens of recipe cards were organized with meticulous care, each one written in the same elegant script she recognized from Mabel's unfinished letter.

The compass sitting on the counter beside them suddenly began spinning, its needle rotating faster as if stirred by an unseen hand. Nora and Maddox exchanged glances as it gradually slowed and returned to pointing north.

"Cinnamon rolls," she read from the first card. "Two cups flour, one-half cup sugar, warm milk, butter ..." She looked up at Maddox. "This is her recipe, the one we keep smelling."

"What else is in there?"

Nora flipped through the cards, reading titles aloud. "Apple Brown Betty, Molasses Cookies, Shepherd's Pie, Fish Chowder ..." She stopped, her breath catching. "Maddox, look at this."

Tucked between the recipe cards were several folded pieces of paper that clearly weren't recipes. The same elegant handwriting, but the tone was different—these were journal entries, domestic observations mixed with personal concerns.

Unlike the unfinished letter she'd found in the basement chest—the one meant for Elias that she'd never been able to send—these journal entries were Mabel's private thoughts, her personal record of daily life and growing concerns.

Nora read aloud.

June 15, 1871. Made Elias's favorite gingerbread for his return from Boston. He says I spoil him, but I cannot help myself when he looks so pleased with my baking. Our neighbor, Mrs. Strout, stopped by and mentioned that Virgil Hawkins has been asking questions about our household—

when Elias is home, when he's expected back from voyages. I
find this presumptuous and told her so.

"Virgil Hawkins," Maddox repeated, his voice tight
with excitement. "Keep reading."

July 2, 1871. That Mr. Hawkins came by today with some
excuse about needing to speak with Elias about shipping
routes. When I told him Elias was at sea, he lingered far too
long, asking when I expected him back and whether I ever felt
lonely in this big house. His manner made me uncomfortable.

"Hawkins again," Maddox said, the name sharp in the
quiet kitchen.

Nora continued reading, growing more tense as the
entries progressed. The pattern that emerged was
disturbing—Virgil Hawkins making repeated visits to the
house when Elias was away, always with some official
excuse, always pushing boundaries and making Mabel
uncomfortable.

August 20, 1871. Mr. Hawkins appeared at my door this
afternoon during the thunderstorm, claiming he needed shel-
ter. I admitted him against my better judgment, but when the
storm passed, he made no move to leave. He stood too close
when I served him tea, and when I moved away, he followed
me about the kitchen, commenting on how well I kept house
and how fortunate Elias was to have such a devoted wife. His
attention felt improper.

"More like predatory," Nora added, then continued.

I was much relieved when the storm ended, and I could
insist he return to his duties.

"He was stalking her," Nora said, filled with disgust.

"And it was escalating," Maddox added grimly. "What else is there?"

Nora flipped through more entries, watching the pattern intensify. Virgil's visits became more frequent, his behavior more presumptuous. Mabel's discomfort grew into fear.

September 25, 1871. I must speak to Elias about Mr. Hawkins when he returns. The man came by today ostensibly to deliver a message about lighthouse maintenance, but his true purpose was clear.

Maddox interrupted. "The lighthouse!" He set his satchel on the kitchen table and shuffled through papers until he found what he was looking for. "Look at this in the lighthouse work records. Virgil Hawkins was on the schedule." Stunned, he sank into a kitchen chair. "As assistant lighthouse keeper."

Nora exchanged looks with Maddox, then continued to read.

He commented extensively on my appearance, saying I looked pale and asking if I was eating properly. When I turned to prepare his tea, I felt his eyes on me in a way that made my skin crawl. He lingered by the kitchen window, watching me work, and made several remarks about how lonely I must be with my husband away so often. I fear his intentions are not honorable.

October 1, 1871. Mr. Hawkins has become increasingly bold. He arrived today without any official business, claiming he was concerned about my welfare during Elias's absence. He brought me a small bouquet of wildflowers, which would have been a kind gesture from anyone else but felt sinister

*coming from him. When I thanked him politely but did not
invite him in, he pushed past me anyway, saying the weather
looked threatening and he should check that all my windows
were properly secured. He spent nearly an hour 'inspecting'
the house, though I suspect he was really studying the layout
and my daily routines.*

"Here's October 3," Nora said softly. "The day of the
shipwreck."

*October 3, 1871. The most terrible day. Mr. Hawkins
came to the door this morning in a state of agitation,
claiming urgent lighthouse business. When I told him Elias
was expected to return today on the evening tide, his expression grew dark and strange. He pushed into the kitchen,
backing me against the counter, and said things no decent
man should say to a married woman. He spoke of his feelings
for me, of how he had watched me and waited, of how Elias
did not deserve such a wife. When I tried to move away, he
grabbed my wrist and said that perhaps it was time for a
change, that men like Elias who took such risks at sea did not
always make it safely home. His words chilled me, but I
thought them merely the ravings of a man whose affections
had been refused. I managed to break free and ordered him
from my house. He left, but not before saying that he would
see me again soon, when circumstances had changed. I pray
Elias returns safely tonight. Mr. Hawkins's manner has filled
me with dread.*

The kitchen fell silent except for the sound of their
breathing. The implications of Mabel's words hung heavy
in the air between them.

"That was a threat," Nora said, her voice shaking.

"And that same night, Elias died," Maddox added, his face pale.

Nora's heart quickened as she considered the implications.

Maddox began searching through the files in his satchel and muttered, "He would have been there. So where is his witness testimony? Next to Shaw, he would've been the most crucial witness."

While Maddox thumbed through more documents, Nora spied an entry on the witness list. "Because he wasn't there. He's listed, but there's a note that he was out of town at the time of the storm."

Maddox frowned. "An alibi. How convenient."

Nora gasped. "The man!" Their eyes locked. "Someone saw a man leaving the lighthouse during the storm. But he didn't walk hunched over like Jasper Shaw."

Maddox nodded. "Because it was Virgil Hawkins."

They stared at each other across Mabel's recipe box. All the pieces were suddenly falling into place—Virgil's unhealthy obsession Mabel, his threat against Elias, his access to the lighthouse, and his presence there on the night of the wreck.

"He lied about being out of town, because he did it," Maddox breathed. "Virgil Hawkins sabotaged the lighthouse. He let the light go out so the *Steadfast* would crash because he was obsessed with Mabel. He murdered Elias and six other men."

"And Mabel must have suspected," Nora added, looking down at the journal entries. "Maybe not exactly what he'd done. No one ever confirmed that the lighthouse beam went out, but she knew Hawkins was dangerous, and she tried to warn Shaw."

The vanilla-cinnamon scent that had been growing stronger throughout their discovery suddenly intensified, filling the kitchen with warmth. The feeling was so strong that Nora looked around the room, half-expecting to see Mabel herself standing there.

"It's like she's been leading us to this," Nora said softly. "All of it—the rolling pin that first night, the scent getting stronger when I'm near her baking utensils, the way I found the chest in the basement, and now this. She's been guiding us to the truth."

"She wanted someone to know," Maddox agreed, his voice filled with wonder and grief. "She lived with the knowledge that Virgil had threatened Elias, and then he died that same night. She must have suspected something, but she had no proof, no one to tell who would believe her."

"And then she died too, carrying that secret."

They stood in the moonlit kitchen, surrounded by Mabel's baking implements and recipes, finally understanding the full tragedy of what had happened that night. It wasn't just a maritime accident or even simple sabotage —it was a crime of lust and jealousy that had destroyed multiple lives and left the truth buried for generations.

Maddox sank into one of the kitchen chairs, running his hands through his hair. "If Virgil really did this ... seven men died because one twisted individual couldn't accept rejection. He would have just ... stood there. Watched the *Steadfast* crash on the rocks, listened to their cries for help." His voice broke slightly. "My great-great-grandfather would have been fighting to save his ship and his crew in that storm, and all the while, the man who could have guided them safely to port might have been watching from the lighthouse, letting them die."

Nora felt tears sting her eyes as she looked down at Mabel's journal entries. "And if we're right about this, Mabel feared something terrible was going to happen but had no way to stop it." She touched the delicate hand-writing with gentle fingers. "Can you imagine living with that fear? Every day wondering when Hawkins would come back, and what he'd do next? And then if Virgil really did cause the wreck ... Elias died that very night, and she would have had to carry the suspicion with her, the terrible possibility that Hawkins's threat had been real."

"Which is why she tried to document his behavior," Maddox said, his voice thick with emotion. "These journal entries—she was probably planning to tell Elias when he returned, to warn him about Virgil's threats. But he never came home."

"And then the whole town blamed him for the wreck. Called him reckless and careless. She had to listen to people destroy her husband's reputation while carrying this terrible doubt that she couldn't prove." Nora wiped away a tear. "No wonder she couldn't survive the grief. It wasn't just losing her husband—it must have been devastating to watch his memory destroyed while suspecting the real killer walked free."

They sat in silence, absorbing it all.

"We have to prove it," Nora said finally, her voice strong with determination. "We have to find evidence that connects Virgil Hawkins to the lighthouse sabotage. For Elias, for Mabel, and for all of them."

Maddox nodded, straightening in his chair as his historian's mind began working through the next steps. "Now that we know who we're looking for, we need to trace his movements after the wreck. Did he stay in Mariner's Bluff? Move away? There should be employment records, maybe boarding house registrations."

Nora's pulse raced as she thought through their next steps. "Where would we find those kinds of records?"

"County courthouse, probably. Birth and death certifi-

cates, maybe probate records if he left any property."
Maddox stood and began pacing again, his excitement
building. "Medical records from that era might be harder to
find, but if he moved to a larger city, there could be hospital
admissions, physician notes."

Nora brightened. "Census records! Let me go get my
laptop." She returned and began searching online. Within a
minute, she'd subscribed to a genealogy website. "Here it
is! The 1880 census shows him in Bangor, Maine."

Maddox didn't share her excitement. "That's a big gap
—nine years after the shipwreck."

Nora tried to stay hopeful. "I know. But it narrows it
down. Bangor might have more records that help us."

Maddox's cautious expression brightened. "It's a start."

Nora said, "It's the best lead we have. Since Hawkins
disappeared right after the shipwreck we'll start with the
census that shows him in Bangor, and we'll work our way
back."

Nora looked around the kitchen at Mabel's recipe box
and the mysterious baking implements that had appeared
to guide them, and she grasped Maddox's hand. "We're
going to find him."

He gazed into her eyes, determined. "The truth needs to
come out."

CHAPTER TWELVE

Two Days Later

Nora made coffee and settled at the kitchen counter, where yesterday's mail still sat in a neat pile along with the contract from Paisley Crawford's agency in New York. The sight made her stomach tighten with anticipation and dread. She'd been avoiding the contract and the offer it represented, but it wasn't going away. So she picked it up.

This deal would put Nora's coastal cottage paintings on everything from coffee mugs to throw pillows, distributed nationwide through major retail chains. The advance was substantial, the royalty percentages generous, and there was a yellow sticky note attached in Paisley's handwriting.

This is even better than we hoped! You're welcome. Just sign this and give me a call when you're ready to celebrate!

- P

Nora set the contract aside. She'd deal with it later.

Right now, all she wanted was to see Maddox again and to follow the leads they'd discovered about Virgil Hawkins.

She grabbed her purse and keys, eager to meet Maddox for their research trip to Bangor.

The drive took them through two hours of winding Maine roads where the landscape changed from coastal pines to inland farms and forests. Specks of autumn color were beginning to blaze against the bright morning sky. When they passed the brick buildings of the University of Maine campus in Orono, Nora glanced over at her passenger.

"Do you miss teaching?" she asked.

Maddox was quiet for a moment.

"I do. But you know what the worst part about losing my job was?" he said finally, his voice careful and controlled. "It wasn't the career stuff—it was my parents' reaction. My dad just sighed and said, 'Well, maybe now you can find something practical.' Like everything I'd worked for was just … an expensive hobby."

The pain in his voice made her heart ache. "They didn't understand what it meant to you."

"They came to exactly one of my academic presentations in five years. Left halfway through because my mother said listening to me talk about dead sailors was 'morbid.'" He laughed, but there was no humor in it. "But they never missed one of my cousin's real estate seminars."

"That must have been crushing."

"I think I threw myself into Elias's story because I understood what it felt like to be misjudged. To have people think the worst of you when you know the truth is different."

He paused, a shadow crossing his face. "Although, actually, it started when I was in fifth grade. We had this assignment to tell a family story, and this kid—Billy Barlow, I'll never forget his name, the little weasel—got up and told the whole class about his ancestor who died in a shipwreck. Made it sound so dramatic and heroic, you know? All the kids were fascinated."

He grew quieter. "Then he said, 'And the captain, Hale's ancestor, was so desperate to get home that he sailed right into a storm and killed everyone on the ship.' I just sat there, feeling everyone staring at me, knowing that was my family he was talking about. The teacher didn't know what to say."

"That must have been devastating for a ten-year-old."

"I went home crying, and when I asked my grand-mother about it, she just looked so sad and said, 'People don't always understand the whole story, Maddox.' That's when I first started reading everything I could about the shipwreck. I guess I've been trying to prove Billy Barlow wrong ever since."

Nora reached across the console and briefly touched his hand. "You know what I think? I think you're the only one in your family who understands what loyalty really means. You've spent five years fighting for someone who can't fight for himself. That's admirable."

She paused, then added quietly, "Maybe they don't deserve the kind of devotion you're showing Elias."

Maddox's eyes widened in surprise, gratitude, or maybe wonder that someone finally understood. The moment hung between them, intimate and honest, before he cleared his throat and looked out at the passing trees.

"What about you?" he asked. "What made you want to be an artist? I mean, before all the commercial stuff?"

Nora felt the familiar tightness in her throat that always came with this memory. "When I was eight, my mom was going through chemo," she began, sounding steadier than she'd expected. "Really bad days, you know? She couldn't keep much down, couldn't sleep.

"We went to stay at my grandmother's house. I would sit by her bed and draw these elaborate fantasy worlds—castles floating on clouds, underwater kingdoms, forests made of candy. There was this painting of the sea on the wall, just a simple seascape, nothing fancy, but when the pain got really bad and she couldn't focus on my drawings, I'd look at that painting and imagine myself there. On a little sailboat on a beautiful sunny day, so free and peaceful."

"She must have loved your drawings."

"She'd study each one like it was the most important thing in the world. She'd ask about every detail—who lived in the castle, what the mermaids ate, why the candy trees grew in spirals. For those minutes, we were both some-where else."

Nora's vision blurred. She blinked hard and focused on the road ahead. "She died when I was ten. And for the longest time, I couldn't draw anything imaginary. It felt too … hopeful, I guess. Too much like the pretend worlds we used to visit together."

"But you kept thinking about that seascape."

"It was a place I could go to, you know? And it stuck. Maritime scenes still bring me back to that place and the idea that you can just sail away."

Her voice caught, and she turned to look through her tears at the passing Maine countryside.

Without a word, Maddox reached over and placed his hand gently on hers, where it rested on her knee.

They drove the rest of the way to Bangor in companion-able quiet, both lost in their own thoughts but somehow more connected than they had been before. The landscape outside changed from rural to suburban to urban, and by the time they reached the city limits, both of them felt ready to tackle whatever they might find.

"Where do we start?" Nora asked as they navigated through downtown Bangor's morning traffic.

"The Bangor Public Library," Maddox said. "They have the best genealogy database in the region, plus digitized city directories and newspaper archives. If Virgil Hawkins lived here, we're bound to find traces of him."

The library was a handsome brick building that housed an impressive genealogy section, with computer terminals, microfilm readers, and helpful librarians who clearly knew their way around historical research.

"We're looking for information about a man named Virgil Hawkins," Maddox explained to the reference librarian, a woman in her fifties with intelligent eyes and an efficient manner. "He would have lived in Bangor sometime between 1871 and 1880."

"Census records would be your best starting point," she said, leading them to a bank of computers.

The librarian said, "We have 1870 and 1880 digitized, plus city directories, vital records, and newspaper archives. Let me show you how to search the databases."

Within minutes, they were deep in the digital archives of 19th-century Bangor. The first hit came quickly—almost too quickly.

"There," Nora said, pointing at the screen. "The same entry we saw online. 1880 Census. Hawkins, Virgil, age 34, occupation listed as 'laborer,' boarding house on Center Street."

Maddox leaned closer, his excitement palpable. "Center Street." He pulled up an image on Google Maps. "From the looks of it, it might have been a working-class district, lots of boarding houses for transient workers."

"Look at this," Nora said, clicking to expand the record. "No family listed, no next of kin. Just him, alone."

They printed the census record and moved on to the city directories. The pattern that emerged was troubling—sporadic employment, frequent moves within the same neighborhood, and gaps in the records that suggested either unemployment or activities he didn't want officially documented.

"1872 Bangor Directory," Maddox read aloud. "Hawkins, V., residence 47 Center Street."

Maddox said, "Remind me to drive past it later."

With a nod, Nora continued. "1873, no listing. 1874 … no listing. 1875 … here he is again. Same address. That's a lot of gaps. Either he wasn't working, or he was working under a different name."

"Or doing work he didn't want recorded," Maddox said grimly.

Then a breakthrough seemed close. Death certificates from the 1870s had been digitized as part of a state historical preservation project. Nora spotted it first with a sharp intake of breath that drew Maddox's attention to her screen. "Here it is. Virgil Hawkins. Date of death: March 15, 1881."

Maddox moved closer. "From what?"

Nora moaned. "They're not accessible online. 'Access to birth, death, and marriage records will now be limited to the person on the record, the person's spouse, registered domestic partner, parent, guardian, descendant…' Well, it goes on and on, but you get the idea."

"Yeah, we're none of those things to Virgil Hawkins." Maddox rubbed his temples.

She took a moment, drew in a deep breath, and then said, "It's okay. We'll just do this the old-fashioned way." Nora closed the laptop. "City Hall, paper forms, and desperate face-to-face pleading."

Maddox grimaced, but began packing up.

BANGOR CITY HALL was a granite fortress of bureaucratic efficiency, all marble floors and echoing footsteps. The vital records office occupied a corner of the first floor. Behind a reception counter stood a woman who looked like she'd been deflecting improper requests since the Carter administration.

Maddox whispered to Nora, "Let me do the talking. This might call for my signature charm."

Her nameplate read "Mrs. Beatrice Curtis, Records Clerk," and her silver hair was arranged in an immovable helmet that suggested she had no patience for nonsense.

Maddox looked into her eyes and smiled. "Hello, I wonder if you could help us. We're looking for a death certificate for—"

"Death certificate request form," she said as she slid a clipboard across the marble surface. "Fill this out completely. You'll need a photo ID, and the processing fee is fifteen dollars. Cash, check, or credit card."

Maddox filled out the form carefully and handed it back. Mrs. Curtis examined it through reading glasses that hung from a chain around her neck.

"Relationship to deceased?" she asked, pen poised over a checklist.

"Well, we're not actually related—"

"Then you can't have the record." She handed the form back without ceremony. "Next."

"Wait," Maddox said, leaning slightly against the counter with a smoldering look that would have made a lesser woman weak in the knees. "This is for historical research. The man died in 1881."

"It doesn't matter if he died in 1781. Rules are rules." Mrs. Curtis said with practiced finality.

Maddox maintained his composure and said gently, "Surely there must be some provision for researchers? Academic institutions?"

"What academic institution are you affiliated with?"

"Uh, none, exactly."

"Then no." Mrs. Curtis looked past them toward the line that was forming behind them. "Next."

Maddox didn't move. Instead, he placed both hands flat on the counter. "Mrs. Curtis," he said with a warm smile, "May I call you Beatrice?"

She looked up at him over her glasses. "Mrs. Curtis will do."

Nora winced. This clearly wasn't the woman's first charm offensive.

Maddox shifted his weight. "Mrs. Curtis, I understand you have rules to follow, and I respect that completely. But we're talking about a man who died a century and a half ago. He has no living relatives, no one who could possibly be harmed by releasing this information." He continued in an easy, conversational tone, as if they were discussing weekend plans rather than bureaucratic policy. "We're trying to solve a historical mystery that's been troubling the people in Mariner's Bluff since 1871. This death certificate could help us understand what really happened during one of the worst maritime disasters in Maine history."

Mrs. Curtis's pen had stopped moving. She was listening.

"I know you deal with people trying to get around the rules every day," Maddox continued. "People fishing for information they shouldn't have, trying to dig up family secrets and cause trouble. But look at this case—1881. There's no one left to protect except the reputation of my great-great-grandfather who lost his life in that shipwreck. This is Nora Delaney. She's an artist who just moved into the ship captain's house and ..."

Mrs. Curtis peered intently at Nora. "Nora Delaney, the artist? Cozy Christmas Teacup Collection!"

A stunned Nora said, "Yes."

In an instant, Beatrice Curtis's face bloomed into a warm grin. "I have two complete sets, and I gave one to my daughter for Christmas. It's a prized possession in our home!"

"Why thank you! Thank you so much!" Nora said sincerely.

Mrs. Curtis slid her reading glasses down long enough to study them over her glasses, and then dashed off a note on a piece of scratch paper. With her game face back on, Mrs. Curtis slid the note to Nora, looked past them, and said firmly, "Next?"

Nora glanced at the note, hooked her arm into a confused Maddox's arm, and tugged him toward the door. Once outside, she gave Maddox the note. "Come back after the last person in line has gone."

Twenty minutes later, they returned as instructed. Mrs. Curtis pulled a file folder from under the counter and slid it to Nora. "This never happened." With a wink, she sent them on their way.

They waited until they were outside before opening the folder. At the top of the page, Virgil Hawkins's name appeared with devastating clarity. "Nora read, 'Age: 35. Cause of death: Laudanum overdose.'"

They stared at the paper in stunned silence. After all their theorizing, all their careful construction of possibility and motive, here was the smoking gun delivered with bureaucratic efficiency.

"Laudanum," Maddox breathed.

"Next of kin: none listed," Nora continued reading. "Address at time of death: 47 Center Street. Attending physician: Dr. Samuel Leighton."

"Leighton," Maddox said, sitting back in his chair. "Hold on." He pulled out his phone and scrolled through his research notes. "Here—You met Captain Joe. His great-grandfather, Thomas Leighton, was the fisherman who saw the lighthouse go dark. I wonder if Dr. Samuel Leighton was his son? In any event, we need to get back to the library to look for his medical records."

BACK AT THE library reference desk, the woman who'd helped them before said, "Oh yes. Dr. Samuel Leighton was one of Bangor's most prominent physicians in the 1870s. His estate donated his practice records to the Bangor Historical Society."

Nora and Maddox exchanged glances.

"Are those records available to researchers?" Maddox asked.

"Oh yes, the Historical Society is just a few blocks from here. They're open until four today. I can call ahead if you'd like."

Minutes later, they were sitting in the climate-controlled archives of the Bangor Historical Society, white cotton gloves on their hands, carefully examining Dr. Samuel Leighton's patient records from the 1870s. The handwriting was precise, the observations clinical, and the story they told was devastating.

"Patient: Virgil Hawkins," Nora read from the first entry, dated December 1881.

Age: approximately 35. Complaints of persistent sleeplessness and nervous exhaustion. Prescribed small dose of
laudanum for sleep.

"January 1872," Maddox continued from the next entry.

Patient returns requesting a stronger medication. Reports
nightmares and persistent anxiety. Patient exhibits signs of
dependency. Request denied.

March 1872: Patient exhibits worsening signs of dependency. Reports unsuccessful attempts to reduce laudanum
dosage. Patient reports guilt over past actions affecting his
sleep.

June 1872: Patient missed two appointments. When seen,
appeared agitated and thin. Reported continued laudanum
use. Counseled regarding dangers of excessive use.

The entries continued chronologically, painting a picture
of a man slowly destroying himself with guilt and
laudanum. Dr. Leighton's notes became increasingly
concerned, documenting missed appointments, erratic
behavior, and what he delicately termed "obsessive
thoughts regarding maritime disasters."

"Look at this one," Nora said softly.

October 1874: Patient in severe distress, spoke repeatedly
of men who died because of his actions. When pressed for
details, became agitated and left without completing
examination. Fear he may be planning self-harm.

"And the final entry," Maddox said, his voice tight with
emotion.

March 1875: Called to examine body of Virgil Hawkins, found deceased in lodgings. Apparent overdose of laudanum. Patient had been taking laudanum against medical advice for some time. Left possible suicide note reading:

God help me. I gave Shaw a sleeping draught and extinguished the beacon. The blood from the Steadfast is on my hands. God forgive me. I did it for love.

They sat in the archives' quiet atmosphere as a 150-year-old truth settled over them. Here, in Dr. Leighton's precise medical handwriting, was Virgil Hawkins's dying confession, a testimony to the unbearable guilt that slowly killed him.

"We did it," Nora whispered.

"We found the truth," Maddox said, his voice rough with emotion. "Elias was innocent. Completely, utterly innocent. And we can prove it."

He stood abruptly and walked to the archive window and looked out at downtown Bangor.

"Maddox," Nora said

He turned back to her, and she saw tears in his eyes— not sadness, but overwhelming relief and joy.

"Five years," he said, his voice breaking slightly. "And it's finally over."

She stood and crossed to him, not thinking about propriety or professional distance or the fact that they were in a public archive. She wrapped her arms around him, and he held her tightly as if she were the only solid thing in a world that had suddenly shifted beneath his feet.

"He was innocent," he murmured against her hair. "And I haven't been mad, after all."

"No, you were right," she said fiercely. "About everything."

They held each other in the quiet archive room, surrounded by the careful documentation of other people's lives and deaths, while outside the afternoon light cast its last glowing warmth of the day.

When they separated, Nora felt tears in her eyes. "Let's go home."

"Let's." His smile was brilliant, transformative. "Captain Elias Wheeler has waited a century and a half for the truth—and now we can tell it."

CHAPTER THIRTEEN

THE DRIVE back from Bangor passed in a blur of exhausted satisfaction. They had actually done it. After 150 years, they had proof that Virgil Hawkins was a murderer and Elias Wheeler was innocent. The evidence sat in a manila folder on the back seat like a bomb waiting to explode the historical record.

"I keep thinking I'm going to wake up and find out we imagined the whole thing," Nora said as they pulled into Maddox's driveway. The sun was setting behind the pine trees, painting everything in shades of deep green and amber.

"Dr. Leighton's medical records were real," Maddox said, though his voice carried the same disbelief. "Hawkins's death certificate was real. The guilt, the laudanum addiction, the note about making amends for deaths at sea—all of it was real."

"But why didn't Dr. Leighton report it? Even ten years late would've been better than nothing."

Maddox said, "Doctor-patient confidentiality."

"But he was dead."

With a nod, Maddox said, "It extends beyond death."

Nora's heart ached for the doctor. "The poor man! Imagine having to keep such a secret from his own home town community."

Maddox narrowed his eyes. "It makes me wonder how Joe's family seemed so sure that Elias was innocent. I wonder if somehow the good doctor was able to convince them without divulging his secret."

Nora sighed. "I suppose there are some things that will never know. And then there's Jasper Shaw and his wife. He never knew he'd been drugged. He thought he'd fallen asleep on duty. The poor man was riddled with guilt for the rest of his life."

"So the torn page must have been her confession that her husband had fallen asleep on the job." Maddox shook his head slowly. "So many lives torn apart by one act."

As they drove back into town, they felt the day's toll. The research had been intense, emotional, and draining despite the positive outcome. Now they needed to decompress and let their minds catch up with what they'd discovered.

A familiar banner stretched across Main Street advertising the annual Mariner's Bluff Chowder Festival for the following day.

"That's making me hungry," Maddox said, glancing at the banner. "Are you hungry? We completely skipped lunch."

"Starving," Nora admitted.

After grabbing some Chinese food, they went to Maddox's cottage and spread out the food and their files to review all their findings.

"Look at this timeline," she said, arranging documents chronologically. "October 3, 1871—Hawkins threatens Elias and Mabel, the shipwreck happens. October 10th—

Hawkins suddenly leaves his lighthouse job without notice. December 1871—he's in Bangor, seeing Dr. Leighton for the first time, complaining of nightmares and sleeplessness."

"And then the slow spiral," Maddox added, handing Nora a plate. "Years of increasing guilt, increasing laudanum use, until he finally overdosed in that boarding house room."

"Alone," Nora said quietly. "No friends or family. Just the gravity of what he had done."

They ate and worked, sorting evidence and building their case with the methodical care of professional historians. But underneath the intellectual satisfaction was something else—a growing awareness of each other, of the partnership that had made this discovery possible, of the connection that had been building between them since that first night when Maddox had appeared on her doorstep with his broken pocket watch.

"We should celebrate," Maddox said as they finished organizing the last of their evidence. "I mean, we just solved one of Maine's oldest maritime mysteries. That deserves some kind of recognition."

"What did you have in mind?"

"Well, tomorrow's the annual Mariner's Bluff Chowder Festival. Good food, live music, half the town turns out. It might be exactly what we need after today—something light and fun to decompress."

Nora smiled. "That sounds perfect. I could use some normalcy after digging through 150-year-old guilt and death certificates."

"The chowder festival it is, then. Fair warning—it's pure small-town Maine at its best. You'll probably meet the other half of the town's population you haven't met yet."

THE NEXT MORNING dawned crisp and clear. The festival was being held in the harbor park, with white tents scattered across the green space and the smell of competing chowders filling the air. Local bands played on a small stage, children ran between the booths with sticky fingers and wide grins, and nearly everyone Nora had met since arriving in town seemed to be there.

"I love it!" she said, watching a group of fishermen argue good-naturedly about whose chowder recipe was superior.

"Wait until you try Mrs. Taylor's clam chowder," Maddox said, guiding her toward a tent where an elderly woman was ladling thick, creamy soup into paper bowls. "She's won the contest three years running, and she's fierce about protecting her recipe."

They spent the afternoon wandering between booths, sampling different chowders, listening to the local high school jazz band, and gradually letting go of the intensity that had carried them through their research. Nora relaxed completely for the first time since arriving in Maine. As she watched Maddox joke with people he'd known since childhood, she felt welcomed by a community that had already started to feel like home.

"You know what I realized today?" she said as they shared a piece of blueberry pie from the Methodist church booth.

"What's that?"

"I've been doing what other people wanted my whole adult life. In New York, I was painting what would fit into neat commercial categories and sell. Even here, I got so caught up in Mabel and Elias's tragedy that I haven't taken much time for myself."

Maddox set down his fork, giving her his full attention. "And now?"

"Now I think maybe I've been living my own life all along. I just didn't recognize it." She gestured toward the surrounding festival, the harbor beyond, and the town that had welcomed her. "This is my life. The house, the mystery, you—all of it. I don't feel like I'm visiting anymore. I'm just living the way I've always wanted to live."

Maddox's eyes softened. "I'm glad you're here, Nora."

"I am, too." She lost herself in the warmth of his gaze.

He was quiet for a moment, watching a group of children chase seagulls near the water. "You know what's funny? I spent five years fighting to clear Elias's name, but I think I was really fighting to prove that caring about something deeply isn't a character flaw. Loyalty, persistence, and pursuing the truth are good things."

"Yes, they are."

"But I was beginning to succumb to other people's doubt. Now I truly believe in myself." He looked at her directly, his eyes serious. "You helped me get to this place."

The afternoon wore on, but neither of them seemed eager to leave. As the sun began to sink toward the horizon, the crowd started to thin. Parents gathered up tired children, elderly couples headed home for early dinners, and the festival took on the quieter, more intimate feeling of a day winding down.

"Want to take a walk?" Maddox asked, nodding toward the path that led along the bluffs above the harbor. "There's something I want to show you."

They climbed the gentle slope that led away from the festival, following a well-worn trail that hugged the coastline. The sound of music and laughter faded behind them, replaced by the eternal rhythm of waves against rocks and the cry of gulls overhead. The path wound through stands of pine and birch, offering glimpses of the harbor below and the endless expanse of the Atlantic beyond.

"This is Mariner's Walk," Maddox explained as they followed the trail. "It was built in the 1920s as a memorial to all the fishermen and sailors lost at sea. Every family in town contributed something—labor, materials, money. It was a true community effort."

"It's beautiful," Nora said, pausing to look out over the water. From this height, she could see the whole harbor spread out below them—the working boats at their moorings, the lighthouse standing sentinel on its rocky point, the town climbing up from the water's edge in neat rows of houses and shops.

"There's more," Maddox said, leading her further along the path.

They walked in comfortable silence, both of them processing the complete transformation of their understanding about the past and their hopes for the future. The path curved around a bend, and suddenly they were standing on a dramatic promontory that jutted out over the ocean. Below them, waves crashed against granite cliffs with a sound like distant thunder, sending sprays of white foam high into the air.

"Oh," Nora breathed, stopping abruptly. "This is incredible."

The view was spectacular—nothing but ocean stretching to the horizon, the coastline curving away in both directions, and the lighthouse standing guard in the distance. The late afternoon light turned the water into a sheet of deep greenish-blue, and the spray from the waves caught the sun like scattered diamonds.

"This is where I come when I need to think," Maddox said, settling onto a granite boulder that formed a natural bench. "When the research gets too frustrating, when I begin doubting myself, or when I need to remember what matters."

Nora sat beside him, close enough that their shoulders touched. "And what matters?"

"Finding what's constant in a world constantly changing. The ocean doesn't care about human schedules, academic careers, or family disapproval. It just keeps doing what it's always done—taking some people home safely and claiming others for itself. The least we can do is find the truth and respect it, and then do what's right."

They sat watching the waves crash against the rocks below. The salt air was crisp and clean, carrying the eternal scents of seaweed and brine that had drawn sailors to the ocean for millennia. Above them, the sky was beginning to deepen from blue to purple as the first stars appeared.

"Nora," Maddox said quietly.

"Mm?"

"I keep thinking about what we found today. Not just the evidence, but what it means." He turned to look at her, his expression serious. "We proved that seven men died because one person couldn't handle rejection. Mabel lived in fear, and Elias died unaware that his wife was being threatened, and an entire family's reputation was destroyed by lies—two, really. The poor Shaws ..."

"It's heartbreaking."

"But it's also inspiring. We proved that the truth matters, and justice can still be served even if it has to wait for 150 years." He stared off into the distance. "Seeing things through your eyes, through your art and your understanding of what Mabel must have felt—it helped me keep going."

"You would have figured it out on your own."

"No," he interrupted gently. "You have no idea how close I was to quitting. The night I knocked on your door, I'd already decided everyone was right about me being obsessed with ghosts. But you saw something worth fighting for, and that made me see it too."

The waves crashed below them, sending another spray of foam into the air. A fishing boat was making its way across the harbor, heading home after a day's work, its lights beginning to twinkle in the gathering dusk.

"You know what I think?" Nora said, her voice barely audible above the sound of the waves.

"What?"

"I think we were supposed to find each other. Not just for the mystery, but for us." She gestured between them.

The words hung between them like a confession, or perhaps it was a question. Nora felt her heart racing, but not with fear—with the certainty of someone who had finally found what she'd been searching for without knowing what it was.

For a moment, neither of them moved. The ocean crashed below, the wind whispered through the pine trees behind them, and somewhere in the distance, the sound of the festival carried on the evening air. But all of that faded into background noise as Maddox reached up to cup her face in his hands.

"I should warn you, I've been told I'm a mess." His smile faded, replaced by an expression of wonder.

"You can't always believe what you hear," she said softly.

They drew closer as if belonging together had its own gravitational pull. When their lips met, their kiss held the desire and strength that had grown through each moment together. Where their first kiss had been a tentative question, this was a confident answer.

The salt air mixed with the warmth between them, and Nora could feel the certainty in his touch. It had been building since the night they'd fallen asleep together on her couch until, at some point, she knew what she felt for him went far deeper than mere attraction.

Nora's fingers tangled in his hair and Maddox's arms tightened around her waist, pulling her closer against him. Her heart hammered against her ribs as his mouth moved against hers, warm and sure. He was everything she hadn't known she'd been waiting for.

She reveled in the solid warmth of his chest beneath her palms as she pressed closer to him. When he brushed his lips against hers, she made a soft sound and clung closer to him. His hands found her face, her neck, threading through her hair as if he couldn't get close enough.

Time seemed to pause. There was only the crash of waves below, the surrounding wind, and the overwhelming rightness of finally finding where they belonged.

When the kiss eventually ended, Nora buried her face against his neck while Maddox wrapped his arms securely around her. There they stayed until the last light faded from the sky and the first stars appeared overhead.

Below them, the ocean continued its eternal dance with the shore, and in the distance, the lighthouse beam began its nightly sweep over the water—a beacon guiding travelers safely home.

CHAPTER FOURTEEN

NORA WOKE to the lingering memory of Maddox's kiss from the cliff walk. She stretched languidly, replaying his kiss, the way his hands cupped her face, and the feeling of absolute safety in his arms.

Her phone rang, showing Maddox's name, and she answered with a smile in her voice. "Good morning."

"Good morning. Sleep well?"

"Better than I have in months. What about you?"

"The same."

Nora smiled at the warmth in his voice.

He said, "Are you free this morning? I want to go over the evidence one more time before we write the formal presentation."

"I'll be right over."

"Actually, would you mind if I came to you? I want to see those artifacts again in their original setting. Sometimes context helps me think more clearly."

"Of course. I'll put on a fresh pot of coffee."

TWENTY MINUTES LATER, Maddox arrived with his research materials and the smile that never failed to make her heart swell. They spread everything across her dining room table —the timeline, the evidence from Bangor, Martha Shaw's journal, and Mabel's recipe box with its hidden secrets.

"For the presentation, we need to make sure people understand this isn't just academic speculation. Virgil Hawkins was a real person who committed a real crime. And the victims deserve to have their stories told."

They worked for an hour, refining their narrative and discussing how to present the evidence most effectively. Nora watched Maddox as he worked, noting the way his eyes lit up when he explained a particularly important connection and the careful reverence with which he handled the historical documents.

"I need to run upstairs for a minute," Nora said. "Help yourself to more coffee."

As she headed upstairs, Maddox wandered into the kitchen to refill his mug. When he turned to put the milk back into the fridge, his arm brushed against a pile of mail and knocked some of it off the counter.

As he bent down to pick up the papers, the words at the top caught his eye. *Crawford Literary Agency, New York, NY.* Below it, in smaller text: *RETAIL LICENSING AGREEMENT.*

His stomach dropped. A contract from a New York agent. A retail licensing deal that would require her to be in the city for meetings, photo shoots, promotional events. All the practical details of a successful art career that had nothing to do with her new life. Unless this wasn't a new life after all, but merely a temporary retreat.

He set down his coffee mug with trembling hands. Of course she had a life in New York. Of course she'd main-tained her professional connections and kept her options open. He'd been an idiot to think their short time together could compete with the career she'd spent years building.

The house—this beautiful Victorian mansion—it wasn't her new home. It was a vacation getaway, a temporary escape from her successful career while she figured out what to do next. And now she had her answer: a lucrative contract that would elevate her career to where she belonged.

BY THE TIME Nora returned to the kitchen, Maddox had moved back to the dining room and was shuffling papers with sudden urgency.

"Actually," he said without looking up, "I just remembered I promised to help my neighbor move some furniture this afternoon. I should probably head out soon."

"Oh." Nora blinked, surprised by the abrupt change in his demeanor. "I thought we were going to work on the presentation all morning."

"We can finish it later in the week. There's no rush." His voice was carefully neutral and professional. "You probably have other things to take care of, anyway."

"Not really. I was looking forward to spending the day with you."

"Right. Well." He gathered his papers with efficient movements that somehow felt like a rejection. "I'll call you later about scheduling our next work session."

He was gone before she could process what had just happened, leaving her standing in her kitchen. Then she spied the contract on the counter, its pages out of order, and the pieces of mail all askew. *No.*

She rushed out and caught him with his hand on the car

door handle. "Look, Maddox, if this is about the contract ..."

He paused as if bracing himself and then turned. "It was an accident. I knocked your mail off the counter, and when I was picking it up, I couldn't help but see it."

"My agent called. This came out of the blue. It's an opportunity—a big one."

"That's great."

But it was clear from the look in Maddox's eyes that this wasn't good news. "It just happened. I haven't talked to anybody about it. It would mean moving back to New York. Appearances, photo shoots, marketing meetings. The whole commercial art world I thought I was done with."

Maddox went very still. "But it's what you've worked for."

"It was." She looked up at him, searching his face. "At one time."

"Now you're having second thoughts about giving up your career for ... all this."

The words hung between them, sharp and painful. Whatever they had together was new, so new it had barely begun. And yet here they were sidestepping the issue that neither could truly ignore.

She said, "I haven't made a decision."

"But you will." He moved toward his car, his movements suddenly brisk and professional. "It's an amazing opportunity. I'm happy for you."

But happy was the last word Nora would have used to describe him at that moment.

He forced a smile, but it didn't reach his eyes. "Goodbye, Nora."

"Maddox, wait—"

"No, this is ..." He nodded. "This is good." He cast hurt eyes at hers. "It's a good reality check."

"But I haven't taken it yet."

A bitter smile came and went. "Key word—yet."

He got into the car and was gone before she could tell him he'd given her a reason to stay. Instead, he assumed that her career would come first, which it didn't, but she couldn't put it last, either.

If they'd known each other longer, it would have been easier. But whatever they had wasn't strong enough yet to base a decision like this upon. If she stayed or left, it had to be because it was right for her, not for a man she was only beginning to know. And then there was the money. It was an awful lot of money—but she could survive without it.

She wished he'd fought harder for her. But the fact that he gave up so easily was telling. While there may have been something between them, it wasn't enough.

Confused and hurt, Nora climbed the stairs to her studio. Maybe painting would help clear her head.

She set up a fresh canvas and began mixing paints, trying to capture the harbor view that never failed to soothe her. She painted through the afternoon and into the evening, stopping only when the natural light faded and she had to switch on her studio lamps. The painting was unlike anything she'd ever created—luminous, ethereal, filled with peace and hope. She had captured the Maine that she loved.

When she finally set down her brush, she wanted to show Maddox immediately. The truth was, she hoped this might serve as an excuse to get together and work out their problems. She pulled out her phone to call him, but it went straight to voicemail.

"Maddox, it's me. I just painted something I wanted to show you."

Hours passed, but he didn't call her back. She tried

again later that evening, but his phone went straight to voicemail again.

Unable to sleep, she stayed up most of the night adding final details to the painting, perfecting the way the light seemed to emanate from the figures themselves, capturing the profound sense of peace she'd felt during the vision.

By morning, she couldn't wait any longer. The painting was still slightly wet, so she took several high-resolution photos with her phone and drove to Maddox's cottage.

She found him in his yard, halfheartedly raking leaves with the distracted air of someone whose mind was else-where entirely.

"We need to talk," she said without preamble.

He looked up with a distant expression. "Nora."

"I called you three times yesterday. I left messages."

"Sorry. I was … busy."

"Moving furniture for twelve hours?"

A flush crept up his neck, but he didn't answer directly. Instead, he leaned on his rake and studied her face with the expression of someone steeling himself for an unpleasant conversation.

"Okay," he said finally, "to be honest, I needed to think and adjust my expectations."

"What do you mean?"

"I mean I got ahead of myself, and I made some assumptions I shouldn't have made."

He sounded so cold and distant, it hurt. "Assumptions about what?"

"About how long you'd be staying in Maine. I hadn't thought of this as a vacation romance."

"A vacation romance?" Her voice rose with hurt and anger. "Is that what you think this is?"

"An incredible one, but yes." He leaned the rake against a tree and faced her fully with a guarded expression. "Nora, you are an amazing and talented woman. I love that about you. But the same thing I love about you means we can't be together. I'm sorry about yesterday. The contract caught me off guard, but I get it. And I really am happy for you."

His words hung between them.

"Maddox." She said softly with increasing concern.

He smiled, but it looked forced. "On the plus side, it looks like I'll see you on TV."

"Well, no, I don't think you will!" The word burst out of her with more force than she'd intended, and then an unexpected laugh bubbled up from inside. She didn't mean to, but she suddenly felt like a burden had been lifted.

Maddox looked confused and a little offended, as if she were laughing at him.

"Maddox, I'm not taking the contract. I haven't even read the damn thing through because I've been too busy solving mysteries and falling in love."

Maddox went still.

He was quiet for so long, Nora wasn't sure how to react. "Maddox?"

His eyes brightened. "You're falling in love?"

Nora felt such overwhelming joy she could barely contain it. "Well, I wasn't planning on telling you yet. I kind of wanted to play hard to get. But, yes!"

Maddox was slow to smile, as if he didn't dare believe it. "But the contract?"

"My agent sent it hoping I'd sign it, but I couldn't. I just called her and told her I'm declining the offer. I've taken this step to rebuild my life, and I'm not going back."

She pulled out her phone and showed him the photos of her painting. "This is who I really am. I'm a painter. I want to paint what I see. And this is what I saw yesterday in my studio. It's why I moved here. This is home. I'm grateful for the career that I had, but it's time to move on."

"But the money—"

"I have enough money. The house is paid for, and I have savings and investments. I can afford to paint and live the life that I've always longed for." She stepped closer to him, close enough to see the gray eyes that had become so dear to her. "And I can spend time with you—if you want to."

The cautious distance in his expression finally cracked, and she saw the raw relief and love underneath. "I thought you were just passing through, and I was an idiot for falling so hard so fast," he said quietly.

"I'm not going anywhere."

He reached out and drew her against him with the desperation of someone who'd thought he'd lost everything that mattered. When he kissed her, it was with the intensity of a man who didn't take anything for granted.

When their kiss grew more intense, Nora pulled away gently. We might want to stop doing this in your front yard before every woman on your street tries to hire you for their lawn care. She laughed, took his hand, and led him inside the cottage.

CHAPTER FIFTEEN

MADDOX'S LIVING room floor had disappeared beneath layers of evidence, turning his cottage into what looked like a detective's war room. They'd given up on trying to fit everything on his dining table hours ago and had spread out on the carpet instead. Photocopied documents, handwritten notes, printouts of medical records, and photographs of artifacts were arranged in careful piles around them. Two laptops sat open on opposite sides of their makeshift workspace, screens glowing with timeline spreadsheets and presentation slides.

"So," she said, "ready to make history? Tomorrow night, we're going to clear Elias Wheeler's name once and for all."

"We're going to do more than that," Maddox said, his voice filled with quiet certainty. "We're going to make sure that seven men who died that night are finally remembered as the victims they were, not casualties of some captain's poor judgment."

"And Mabel," Nora added softly. "She'll finally be seen as the brave woman who tried to document a dangerous man's behavior, not just a grieving widow."

Maddox nodded, then looked toward his cottage. "Come on. Let's put this thing together."

"Okay," Maddox said, holding up a copy of Dr. Leighton's medical records from where he sat cross-legged among the papers. "This goes in the guilt section, right after we establish the timeline of Hawkins leaving town."

"Right," Nora agreed, then looked up from her own laptop, where she'd been organizing photographs of Mabel's journal entries. "Wait, what did you just say?"

"The medical records. They go after—" He caught the expression on her face and grinned. "You weren't listening to a word I said, were you?"

"I was listening. Sort of." She closed her laptop and crawled across the papers toward him, careful not to disturb their organized piles. "I was mostly thinking about how attractive you look when you're being all brainy and brawny."

"We have a presentation to finish," he said, but his voice lacked conviction as she settled beside him and slipped her arms around his shoulders.

"We have plenty of time," she murmured, leaning in to kiss him. "The presentation isn't until tomorrow night."

"Nora …" But he was already setting down the medical records and turning to face her fully.

"Besides," she said, her fingers toying with the collar of his shirt, "I think we work better when we take breaks."

"Is that what you call this? A break?"

"A very necessary break." She kissed him softly, and he made a sound of surrender that made her smile against his lips.

Their work lay forgotten for several minutes while they held each other among the scattered pieces of evidence. When they finally parted, Maddox rested his forehead against hers.

"We have a presentation to finish, and you are a distraction," he said.

"I'm not a distraction. I'm a motivation."

"Oh, I'm motivated, all right. Just not to do work." He grinned and gestured at the chaos surrounding them. "That evidence isn't going to present itself."

Nora laughed and picked up a photograph of Elias's compass. "Okay, fine. Back to work."

They settled back into their work, laptops balanced on their knees. Maddox would lean over to point out a connection in the timeline, and Nora would brush her hand along his arm as she reached for documents. When she got excited about a particular piece of evidence, he'd set aside whatever he was holding and pull her in for a quick kiss before they returned to organizing papers.

"Here," Nora said, sliding a printed photo across the carpet between them. "The enamel miniature of Mabel from the museum. This should go in the section about her harassment by Hawkins. People need to see her as a real person, not just a name in a historical record."

"Good thinking." Maddox added it to his stack of visual aids. "And we'll pair it with her journal entries about his unwanted visits. Seeing her face and reading her words in her own handwriting will paint a powerful picture of what happened."

"I'm all about painting pictures," Nora said, smiling.

They worked in comfortable silence for a while, the only sounds the clicking of laptop keys and the occasional rustle of papers being moved from one pile to another. The coffee Maddox had made earlier sat forgotten in their mugs, grown cold while they focused on perfecting their presentation.

"Question," Nora said, looking up from a timeline she'd

been reviewing. "When you present the witness testimony about the light going out, should we mention that some of the testimony was discounted because of weather conditions?"

"Absolutely. That's part of what makes this so compelling." Maddox reached for a folder of witness statements. "Thomas Leighton and the others weren't believed because investigators thought the storm made reliable observation impossible. But when you have multiple people reporting the same thing ..."

"It stops being unreliable testimony and becomes part of a pattern."

"Right. And now we know what they were probably seeing—Hawkins leaving the lighthouse after sabotaging the light." He pulled out Leighton's original statement. "So I'll read this aloud so people hear his actual words."

Nora scooted closer to read over his shoulder, her hair brushing his cheek. "He sounds so certain, even with the qualifier about weather conditions."

"Because he was certain. He saw something that night, and it bothered him enough that he reported it even when he knew people might not believe him." Maddox turned his head to look at her, and she was close enough that their noses almost touched. "Kind of like someone else I know who trusted her instincts even when they led her into a 150-year-old mystery."

"Are you comparing me to a crusty old 19th-century fisherman?"

His eyes sparkled. "A much prettier version, someone who saw the truth when everyone else missed it."

She kissed him then, soft and lingering, and then rested her hand on his chest.

"This feels right," she said simply.

"It does." He covered her hand with his. "Even when you make it impossible to concentrate."

"I think we're almost done, anyway." She looked around at the organized piles of documents, the neat stacks of photographs, the laptops displaying their completed timelines. "We just need to scan all of this and format it into a presentation and book manuscript. And then, you're going to change history."

"We're going to change history."

"No," she said firmly. "This is your moment, Maddox. Your vindication. Your triumph. I'll be in the audience, cheering you on, but this presentation belongs to you."

He was quiet for a moment, looking down at her with an expression so tender it made her heart ache.

"What time is it?" Maddox asked suddenly. "I want to make sure we have enough time to practice the whole presentation once more before tomorrow."

Nora glanced toward the coffee table where Elias's pocket watch sat among their other artifacts, and her eyes widened. "Maddox," she said quietly, pointing toward the watch.

The steady, confident ticking was clearly audible now, amplified by the wooden surface of the coffee table. The sound filled the quiet cottage with its rhythmic beat.

They both stared at the watch.

"It's working," Nora whispered.

"It always works at your house, but ..." He stopped, his eyes widening as the realization hit him. "We're not at your house."

They looked at each other across the evidence-scattered floor. Since they'd met, the pocket watch had only ticked when Maddox was on the grounds of the Captain's Watch. It had been their supernatural compass, their connection to Elias's restless spirit.

At Maddox's cottage, for the first time, a watch—whose sound had been absent from his family for generations—ticked steadily, as if Time itself could now finally move on.

CHAPTER SIXTEEN

THE OCTOBER AFTERNOON was crisp and clear, with the kind of brilliant sunshine that made the turning leaves look like stained glass. Chairs were arranged in neat rows along the Mariner's Walk, facing the harbor where the tragedy had unfolded 150 years ago. The lighthouse stood sentinel in the distance, its white tower catching the sunlight, and beyond it stretched the endless blue of the Atlantic.

Nora stood at the back of the gathering, watching as residents of Mariner's Bluff settled into their seats. Mrs. Foster had claimed a front-row chair and was holding court with several other elderly residents, all of them buzzing with excitement about the ceremony. Captain Joe Leighton sat with a group of fishermen, their weathered faces serious and respectful. Even members of the high school string quartet had shown up, their instruments resting nearby, ready to play during the ceremony.

But it was the two figures in the third row that stirred Nora's emotions. Dr. Robert Hale and his wife, Margaret, sat quietly, their faces composed and eyes fixed on their son. An expression of pride and, she hoped, some regret filled their eyes. They had flown up from Florida and appeared at Maddox's cottage that morning, stating simply, "We came to hear you speak."

Maddox stood near the covered memorial plaque and a large screen, looking handsome and effortlessly cool in his navy blazer, crisp Oxford shirt, and dark jeans, but Nora could see the nervous energy in the way he kept checking his notes. This was his moment—the vindication he'd been seeking for five years, the chance to clear his great-great-grandfather's name in front of the community that had shaped both their stories.

Mayor Maxine Lambert stepped up to the small podium that had been positioned near the memorial site. "Friends and neighbors," she began, her amplified voice carrying easily in the crisp air, "we gather today to dedicate this memorial to Captain Elias Wheeler and the crew of the merchant vessel *Steadfast*, lost in the great storm of October 3, 1871."

She paused, looking out over the crowd. "For 150 years, the official record has painted Captain Wheeler as a reckless man whose poor judgment cost seven lives. But recent research by our own Dr. Maddox Hale has revealed a very different story." Mayor Lambert turned to Maddox and smiled. "Dr. Hale will share his findings with us today, but first, let me say that this memorial represents more than just historical correction. It represents our community's commitment to truth, to historical accuracy, and to honoring those who died here seeking safe harbor. And with that, Ladies and gentlemen, Dr. Maddox Hale." She started clapping and stepped aside.

Through the applause, a murmur rippled through the crowd as Mayor Lambert said softly, "Ready, Dr. Hale?"

Maddox approached the podium with steady steps, placing his notes on the lectern. When he looked up at the crowd, his eyes found Nora's first, and she gave him an encouraging nod that seemed to steady him.

He pulled Elias's watch from his jacket pocket, its steady ticking as strong and sure as it had been since that first night at Nora's door. The gold case caught the afternoon light, and for a moment, he could almost feel his great-great-grandfather's presence—not seeking justice anymore, but offering approval.

As he closed the watch with a satisfied click, he began. "It's time we set the record straight."

"Five years ago, most of you probably thought I was a little obsessed with maritime history." A subtle smile played at the corner of his mouth. "Some of you might have been more blunt in your assessment."

A gentle chuckle rippled through the crowd, and Nora saw some of the tension leave his shoulders.

"You weren't wrong," he continued with a self-deprecating smile. "I was obsessed. But sometimes obsession is just another word for commitment. I was determined to uncover the truth."

He turned slightly, gesturing toward the harbor. "On the night of October 3, 1871, seven men died in these waters. The official inquiry blamed their deaths on Captain Elias Wheeler's reckless decision not to shelter sooner, but to press on to our harbor during dangerous weather conditions. For 150 years, that was the accepted story."

Maddox's voice grew stronger, more confident. "But the truth is far different and far more tragic. Captain Wheeler and his crew were not victims of poor judgment—they were victims of murder."

The crowd stirred, leaning forward with renewed attention.

"Through meticulous research, conducted with the invaluable assistance of Nora Delaney—" He nodded toward her, and she felt heat rise in her cheeks as several heads turned in her direction. "—we have uncovered evidence that the lighthouse was deliberately sabotaged that night by assistant lighthouse keeper Virgil Hawkins."

For the next twenty minutes, Maddox laid out their case with the precision of a scholar and the passion of a descendant seeking justice. He spoke of Mabel's journal entries documenting Hawkins's harassment, of witness testimony that had been dismissed, and of medical records showing Hawkins's spiral into guilt and laudanum addiction that ultimately killed him.

"The evidence is overwhelming," he said confidently. "Virgil Hawkins drugged lighthouse keeper Jasper Shaw, then extinguished the lighthouse beam at the crucial moment when the *Steadfast* needed it most. Seven men died that night—not because of Captain Wheeler's recklessness, but because one man's response to rejection was murder."

Nora watched the faces in the crowd as the truth sank in. She saw expressions of dismay, sadness, and a growing sense of outrage that such an injustice had stood uncorrected for so long.

"But this memorial isn't just about correcting the historical record," Maddox continued, his voice growing softer and more personal. "It's about remembering that every life lost at sea represents someone's husband, wife, parent, sibling, or child. Captain Elias Wheeler was on his way home to his pregnant wife, and the members of his crew were returning to their own families. He was a skilled and experienced mariner who trusted the lighthouse to guide him safely to port."

His voice caught slightly. "But the lighthouse he had relied on in so many journeys now failed him through no fault of his own."

Maddox stepped back from the podium and moved to

the covered memorial. With careful hands, he pulled away the cloth, revealing a bronze plaque mounted on a granite stone that faced the harbor. It read:

In Memory of Captain Elias Wheeler, a skilled and respected mariner, and the crew of the merchant vessel *Steadfast*, lost October 3, 1871. Sailors who nobly died seeking safe harbor. They are remembered as victims of man's frailty and the sea's timeless dominion.

For a moment, the only sounds were the cry of gulls and the eternal rhythm of waves against stone. A hundred and fifty years of injustice had finally lifted, replaced by the simple dignity of truth acknowledged.

When the formal ceremony concluded, people lingered to examine the memorial plaque and discuss the revelations among themselves. Nora watched Maddox's parents approach him. "I'm proud of you, son," Dr. Robert Hale said quietly.

His mother stepped forward without words, cupping her son's face in her hands the way she had when he was small, her eyes bright with unshed tears. Nora's eyes misted as she watched Maddox embrace his parents, five years of hurt and misunderstanding finally beginning to heal.

As the crowd gradually dispersed, Nora heard a familiar gravelly voice behind her. "Ayuh, I always knew that house had more stories to tell. Good thing it found the right person to listen." She turned to find Milt Thurlow standing there with his weathered hands clasped behind his back, a satisfied smile on his face.

"Milt!" Nora's face lit up. "I'm so glad you came."

"I wouldn't have missed it," he said, nodding toward Maddox, who was still surrounded by well-wishers. "That young man's done good work. And you too, so I hear."

A moment later, Nora felt another familiar hand on her shoulder. "Surprise," Caroline's voice said behind her.

Nora turned to find her best friend standing there with a sheepish expression. "Caroline! What are you doing here?"

"I drove up this morning. I figured if my best friend was about to witness history being made, I should probably be here." Caroline glanced toward Maddox, who was still surrounded by community members congratulating him. "He's a keeper."

Nora smiled. "I know."

Caroline hooked her arm through Nora's. "Well, aren't you going to introduce me?"

As Maddox finished speaking with a group from the historical society, Hilda approached him. Her eyes were bright with unshed tears.

"Well done, Dr. Hale. Well done."

"Thank you, Hilda. I couldn't have done it without all your help with the records."

Hilda turned to Nora. "You're lucky," she said with a wink. "If I were forty years younger, you'd have some competition on your hands."

As the afternoon wore on, more people stopped to congratulate Maddox or examine the memorial.

"Beautiful work," Mayor Lambert said warmly to Nora.

"Maddox did all the research," Nora said. "I just helped organize the evidence."

"I wasn't talking about the research, though that was impressive too." Mayor Lambert smiled warmly. "I saw the new lighthouse museum display of your maritime paintings. The way you captured Mabel's story, the emotional truth behind the historical facts—it's exactly what we need to help people understand our history. The town council has been discussing commissioning you for some work."

"I'd be honored," Nora said, surprised but pleased by the offer.

"Good. We'll be in touch." Mayor Lambert smiled and moved on to speak with other lingering community members.

As the crowd finally thinned, Nora and Maddox stood alone by the memorial as the sun sank toward the horizon. The harbor spread out before them, peaceful in the evening light, with fishing boats heading home after their day's work. Maddox reached over and clasped Nora's hand.

The October evening was settling into the peaceful quiet that Nora had come to love about coastal Maine. Hand in hand, she and Maddox walked along the cliff path, both still processing the day's events.

The evening mist was beginning to roll in from the Atlantic, softening the edges of the familiar coastline. Waves crashed against the granite cliffs below with their eternal rhythm, and somewhere in the distance, the lighthouse began its nightly sweep across the darkening water.

They had almost reached the promontory where they'd shared their first kiss when Nora caught sight of movement ahead on the path. Through the thickening mist, she could make out two figures walking slowly along the cliff edge— a tall man and a woman who appeared to be holding an infant.

"Do you see—" she began, but Maddox was already nodding.

The figures moved with unhurried grace, the man's arm around the woman's shoulders, both of them gazing down at the child. There was something timeless about the scene, as if they existed in their own pocket of eternity, separate from the living world but sharing the same beautiful coastline.

As Nora and Maddox watched, hardly daring to

breathe, the family ahead seemed to sense their presence. The couple turned, and for just a moment, their faces were visible through the mist—Elias with his storm-gray eyes and gentle smile, Mabel radiant with joy, and between them the baby they'd never been able to hold in life.

The man raised his free hand in a gesture that could have been a greeting or farewell, and the woman smiled with infinite peace. Then they turned back toward the sea and continued their walk along the cliffs where they'd first lived, loved, and lost one another.

The mist swirled thicker, and when it cleared, the path ahead was empty.

Nora and Maddox lingered breathless before heading back toward town as full darkness fell over the coast. The mist had now cleared, leaving only the familiar path ahead and the town lights twinkling in the distance.

Nora smiled and looked at Maddox. "Well, now what will we do with our time?"

Maddox smiled back, but then his expression turned serious and tender. "Live our own lives," he said quietly, "and love."

The distant lighthouse beam swept over the water in its eternal quest to guide travelers home while two people finished one journey and started another.

THE WATERFRONT
SUMMERS COLLECTION

Three waterfront towns. Three women finding their way. Three heartwarming love stories. Can be read in any order.

Three enchanting lakeside and coastal towns. Three women finding their way home. Three love stories that will warm your heart and restore your faith in second chances.

Escape to charming waterfront communities where summer breezes carry the promise of new beginnings, and love has a way of finding you when you least expect it—and need it most.

https://www.jljarvis.com/waterfront/

THANK YOU!

Thank you for reading! If you enjoyed this book, please consider leaving a review or a rating. Your feedback on bookstore, Goodreads, and Bookbub websites helps other readers discover books they'll enjoy.

instagram.com/jljarvis.writer
facebook.com/jljarvis1writer
x.com/JLJarvis_writer
youtube.com/@jljarvis-author
goodreads.com/jljarvis
bookbub.com/authors/j-l-jarvis

ALSO BY J.L. JARVIS

Waterfront Summers

(Can be read in any order)

The Cottage at Peregrine Cove

The House on Serenity Lake

Moonlight on Mariner's Bluff

Drake & Wilde Mysteries

(Reading Order)

Love in the Time of Pumpkins

Secrets in the Hollow

Shadow of the Horseman

Standalones

(Can be read in any order)

A Cowboy Kind of Love

A Christmas Eve Stop

Christmas by Lamplight

A Kiss in the Rain

App-ily Ever After

Once Upon a Winter

The Red Rose

Highland Vow

Short Stories

(Can be read in any order)

The Magic of Snow

The Eleventh-Hour Pact

A Christmas Yarn

The Farmer and the Belle

Work-Crush Balance

Cedar Creek
(Can be read in any order)

Christmas at Cedar Creek

Snowstorm at Cedar Creek

Sunlight on Cedar Creek

Pine Harbor
(Reading Order)

Allison's Pine Harbor Summer

Evelyn's Pine Harbor Autumn

Lydia's Pine Harbor Christmas

Holiday House
(Can be read in any order)

The Christmas Cabin

The Winter Lodge

The Lighthouse

The Christmas Castle

The Beach House

The Christmas Tree Inn

The Holiday Hideaway

Highland Passage
(Can be read in any order)

Highland Passage

Knight Errant

Lost Bride

Highland Soldiers

(Reading Order)

The Enemy

The Betrayal

The Return

The Wanderer

American Hearts

(Can be read in any order)

Secret Hearts

Forbidden Hearts

Runaway Hearts

For more information, visit jljarvis.com.

Get monthly book news at news.jljarvis.com.

ABOUT THE AUTHOR

J.L. Jarvis is a left-handed former opera singer/teacher/lawyer who writes books. She now lives and writes on a mountaintop in upstate New York.

jljarvis.com